That did it! Now he had gone too far!

Isla's voice was brittle as she asked him, "Does your wife know about these intimate scenarios you stage with old girlfriends?"

A shutter seemed to drop down over his eyes. In a strange tone of voice, half earnest, half throwaway, Rory informed her, "I'm not sure I can be classified as a married man. You see, I have no marriage... I have no wife."

An alarm bell sounded in Isla's head. She had heard this kind of claim before. "Are you trying to tell me," she queried frankly, "that that woman you live with is a figment of everyone's imagination?"

"Oh, no, she's real enough," he answered. "But we have no marriage anymore. We may appear to live together, but we are really strangers."

Stephanie Howard is a British author whose two ambitions since childhood were to see the world and to write. Her first venture into the world was a four-year stay in Italy, learning the language and supporting herself by writing short stories. Then her sensible side brought her back to London to read Social Administrations at the London School of Economics. She has held various editorial posts at magazines such as *Reader's Digest*, *Vanity Fair*, and *Women's Own*, as well as writing free-lance for *Cosmopolitan*, *Good Housekeeping* and *The Observer*. She recently spent six years happily trotting around the globe, but has now returned to the U.K. to write.

Books by Stephanie Howard

HARLEQUIN PRESENTS

HARLEQUIN ROMANCE

Don't miss any of our special offers. Write to us at the following address for information on our newest releases.

Harlequin Reader Service
P.O. Box 1397, Buffalo, NY 14240
Canadian address: P.O. Box 603,
Fort Erie, Ont. L2A 5X3

STEPHANIE HOWARD

a bride for strathallane

Harlequin Books

TORONTO • NEW YORK • LONDON
AMSTERDAM • PARIS • SYDNEY • HAMBURG
STOCKHOLM • ATHENS • TOKYO • MILAN
MADRID • WARSAW • BUDAPEST • AUCKLAND

Harlequin Presents first edition April 1992
ISBN 0-373-11450-8

Original hardcover edition published in 1990
by Mills & Boon Limited

A BRIDE FOR STRATHALLANE

CHAPTER ONE

IT WAS a bright winter's day, one week before Christmas, and from the cold North Sea an east wind was blowing, strong enough to blow the ears off a donkey.

Isla climbed out of the car, turned up the collar of her navy cashmere coat and strode purposefully across the tarmac to the main entrance of the Buchanan building. No one would have guessed from her air of poised assurance that, secretly, she was quaking inside.

In the darkly carpeted entrance hall, with its wood-panelled walls, adorned with ornately framed oils, and general air of old wealth and sobriety, she paused for a second to shake her wind-blown hair once more into its habitual immaculate bob, then walked on brisk, unhesitating steps to the high-speed lift beyond the reception desk. She had no need to ask for directions. She knew exactly where she was going.

At her third-floor destination the lift doors reopened. Isla stepped out and headed without a pause for the glass-panelled door which bore the legend, printed in a flourish of gilded lettering, 'Rory Buchanan, Managing Director'. Without bothering to knock, she stepped inside and confronted the young secretary who blinked up at her in astonishment.

'I wish to see Mr Buchanan—now, please,' she demanded.

The girl was momentarily thrown. She could tell at a glance that the young woman before her—with her well-cut navy cashmere coat, stylish accessories and expensive London grooming—was a stranger and, possibly, a person of some importance. In Strathallane one rarely came across such polish.

And as the young secretary paused, uncertain how to respond, Isla smiled wryly to herself. She had known exactly the effect she would have on the young girl. The impact of her unusually striking looks, together with her assured and confident bearing, was something she was well aware of and, indeed, had cultivated with some care. In the past it had opened many doors for her, just as it was about to open another one now. Yet the irony of the situation was not lost on her. The flush-faced, flustered girl before her could have been herself just a few years ago.

The secretary looked up into the beautiful, impassive face, with its perfect pale complexion, violet-coloured eyes and frame of burnished chestnut hair, and, almost apologetically, told her, 'Mr Buchanan never sees anyone without an appointment.'

Isla raised one perfectly pencilled eyebrow, a gesture familiar to her colleagues down south and known for its powers of intimidation. 'Don't worry,' she assured the pink-faced girl. 'I'm sure Mr Buchanan will agree to see me. Just tell him Miss Isla MacDonald is here.'

The raised eyebrow, as ever, worked like a charm. The girl turned to the internal phone on her desk, picked up the receiver and punched a couple of buttons. 'I'm sorry to bother you, sir,' she began, 'but there's a Miss Isla MacDonald here to see you.' As she spoke, she flicked Isla a wary glance. 'I'm afraid she's insisting that she sees you right away.'

There was a pause, a fairly lengthy pause, then the crackle of a reply at the other end of the line.

'Very well, sir.' The secretary laid down the receiver and turned to Isla with a cautious smile. 'He'll see you now. You can go right in.' She nodded towards the door of the inner office—but Isla was already halfway there. A moment later, her head held high, the butterflies in her stomach firmly controlled, she was pushing the door open and stepping boldly into the huge, impressive room beyond.

For a moment all she could see was a vast expanse of carpet with a massive mahogany desk in dark silhouette against the tall windows at the other end. Then, squinting a little against the pale sunlight, she distinguished the dark figure of a man facing her from behind the desk.

The man rose to his feet, his face still in shadow, yet she was fiercely conscious of his eyes upon her as on oddly numb legs she crossed the silent carpet till she was standing right at the edge of his desk.

And now, quite suddenly, she could see him clearly, and just for an instant, as she looked into his face, she felt raw and vulnerable, her heart in flames. In the space of a heartbeat all the years fell away. For an instant it felt as though nothing had changed.

Then the instant passed and, with an effort of will, she had reduced him in her mind to what he really was—a mere distant echo of a long-forgotten era, an unfortunate relic of her past.

She took a deep breath. 'Hello, Rory,' she said.

A pair of eyes the colour of a golden eagle's swept her minutely from head to toe, causing her skin to prickle with uncomfortable awareness, stiffening the hairs on the back of her neck. For a moment he said nothing, then, unexpectedly, he smiled. 'Hello, Isla. You're looking well.'

Eight years had passed, yet he had scarcely altered. Those tawny eyes, that beguiling smile, the straight black brows, the faintly crooked nose. Like herself, he was a little older now, but he was still as devilishly handsome as before.

And yet everything had changed, she reflected with irony as, with a wave of his hand, he bade her sit down. The child she had been then—innocent and eighteen—had vanished forever into the mists of time. In her place sat a poised and sophisticated young woman, the highly successful and respected editor of a London-based glossy fashion magazine. And the wild young man that had been Rory Buchanan, the renegade son, the free-spirited rebel, had been miraculously transformed into a pillar of society.

For the thirty-three-year-old man who stood before her now, dressed in a mid-grey Savile Row suit, his raven-dark hair brushed back from his brow, the spark of shrewd intelligence lighting his eyes, looked every inch the high-powered executive that in less than a decade he had become.

Buchanan of Strathallane, as the locals reverently called him, the title that had been his father's and his grandfather's before him. It was a title to which he did evident justice. Eight years ago few would have believed it.

And there had been other changes, too, equally far-reaching. For Rory was now a married man.

All these thoughts went through Isla's head as she arranged herself in one of the high-backed chairs, and they were thoughts that both cheered and deeply reassured her. The past and the present were forever divided. There was nothing any more that linked the one to the other.

Yet another proof of that was the magnificent manner in which she was currently coping with this ordeal. Apart from that fleeting moment of weakness when she had first looked into his face— a lapse surely to be expected after all these years?— the only emotion she felt for the man before her was one of cold, detached indifference. And that scarcely even qualified as an emotion.

He had resumed his seat behind the desk and was regarding her with frank curiosity. 'So, to what do I owe this unexpected pleasure? I take it you haven't just come here to wish me a Merry Christmas?'

Isla met his smile with a coldly raised eyebrow. 'Indeed I have not,' she assured him condescendingly. The days when that smile of his could melt her heart-strings and turn her will to a lump of soft putty had ended a very long time ago. With his callous treatment of her all those years ago he personally had made sure of that. So he would be wasting his time now if he tried to charm her.

Likewise, she sensed, as she crossed her slim legs, her own 'eyebrow treatment' had for once fallen flat. She had no more hope of intimidating him than he had of charming her. Still, she continued with composure, 'I've come to speak to you on a matter of some importance. I'm here, as a matter of fact, on behalf of my parents.'

Rory raised one black eyebrow as he looked across at her. 'Something to do with your father?' he enquired quickly, his tone tinged with a concern Isla knew he did not feel. 'I heard he'd had a heart attack and that he'd been in hospital, but I understood he was getting better.'

'He is getting better. Much better, thank you.'

'I even heard he was back at work?'

'Only part time,' Isla conceded briskly, regarding him steadily, refusing to be diverted. It was, among other things, the recent illness of her much loved and respected watch-maker father that had brought her north to her native Scotland to spend Christmas and Hogmanay with her parents. But her father's health, which was no concern of Rory's, was not the reason she was here now in his office.

She looked him straight in his unblinking golden eagle's eyes and spelled out to him in uncompromising syllables, 'The reason I'm here is because I want to talk to you about your plans to build in Jock Campbell's field—that piece of land in front of my parents' cottage.' Only an issue of the utmost importance could ever have brought her on this unpalatable mission.

Rory paused a beat, then looked at her blankly. 'What plans, pray, are you talking about?'

Isla had half expected this response. Few people could stonewall as effectively as Rory. She uncrossed her knees pointedly and leaned towards him. 'Don't try to pretend. I know you've bought the land. It's registered under the name of

Cairngorm Holdings, a company which I happen to know belongs to Buchanan's.' Her voice had risen a little with indignation. 'My parents were unaware of it, which was why they didn't know who to complain to, but, fortunately, I remembered that it's one of yours.' She hated him for his deceit and downright deviousness. 'Don't tell me you now have the gall to deny it?'

'That the company is mine? I don't deny that.' A perceptible edge had crept into his voice.

'Then would you deny that you've bought that piece of land directly in front of my parents' cottage?'

'If, as you said, you're referring to Jock Campbell's field, why should I deny it? It was bought on the open market.'

So, finally, she had managed to squeeze the truth from him! 'I congratulate you,' Isla offered with sarcasm. 'For such a prime piece of land you must have paid a good price. I imagine there must have been a fair bit of competition. After all,' she hurried on, her tone suddenly hardening as she reached the nub of the point she was making, 'a piece of land like that, for which building permission has already been granted, doesn't exactly come along every day of the week. You were really very lucky to get it.'

The deep tawny eyes had narrowed to a glitter and beneath the tan of his skin the strong jawbone had tautened. He seemed to bite out the syllables as he told her, 'Luck had really nothing to do with it. I got it because I was prepared to pay the highest price.'

'I'll bet you were!' The words were a condemnation—of what he was, of what he stood for, of every conceivable aspect of him. Hadn't she always known that, whatever Rory wanted, Rory went after and invariably got? He more than likely never even noticed the moans of the crushed who got in his way. But this time she would force him to listen to their protests. 'I suppose you realise what it will mean to my parents if building goes ahead on that piece of land? It will destroy their view, put an end to their privacy and slash the value of their property. That's why I can't let you go ahead with it.'

Rory leaned back in his leather swivel chair, his shoulders broad beneath the fine cut of his jacket, and for an instant, as he seemed to flex his muscles, there was a flash of the wild renegade of earlier days. 'So, that's what you're worried about?' he put to her harshly. 'You're afraid that your patrimony might be devalued.'

Isla smiled inwardly. Smart move! she thought. He's trying to put me on the defensive. But she hadn't made her rise to the top of the tree through the dog-eat-dog ranks of fashion magazine journalism without learning a trick or two herself. The devaluation of her 'patrimony', as he called it, was the very last thing that concerned her. But let him believe of her whatever he pleased. She had no intention of being diverted into trying to convince him of the purity of her motives. Attack, not defence, was the strategy that won arguments!

She glanced down at her perfectly manicured fingernails, then raised her eyes once more to Rory. 'As I understand it, it is you, not I, who has a tendency towards material acquisitiveness these days.' Her inner smile broadened as a flicker crossed his eyes. This was not the reaction he had been expecting.

Beneath the straight black brows the tawny eyes narrowed. 'Would you care to elaborate?' he enquired crisply.

'With pleasure.' Serenely Isla held his gaze as she shook back her cap of glossy chestnut hair. 'You seem to be making a career out of business expansion. Property companies, development corporations—even a research laboratory up in Caithness, I believe. It seems no area of business is too obscure these days to save it from being snapped up by Buchanan's.'

As she was speaking, he had picked up from the leather desk-top an antique bone-handled silver paper-knife. As he weighed it in his hand, it flashed like a stiletto, a flash that was reflected in his eyes as he told her, 'You've missed out the electronic components factory, the haulage contracting company and the fish farming project, not to mention quite a number of other things.' Distractedly he tested the point of the paper-knife against the tip of one long, tanned finger and threw her a look of warning as he added, 'If you want, I can have my secretary prepare you a list.'

Isla attempted to fell him with a look. 'Please don't trouble yourself. I'm really not all that interested.' But neither the look nor her protest seemed to impress him.

'No trouble, I promise you.' He held her eyes. 'Surely it would be the least I could do for an old friend.'

A squeeze of anger shot through her at the studied slight. What was past was past and long forgotten, but wasn't it just typical of what he had become that he should deliberately devalue what their relationship had once been? Old friend, indeed! They had been lovers, not friends. And he had betrayed her as cruelly as only a lover could.

But as their eyes locked like the antlers of two stags in combat she was saved from having to respond to this insult when one of the phones on his desk began to ring.

As he picked it up and began to speak, she watched him from the corner of her eye. She had accused him of greed, of material acquisitiveness, but the truth was that she admired what he had achieved. Eight years ago, when he had inherited Buchanan's, it had been what it had always been for a hundred years—a small provincial publishing house producing no more than half a dozen titles, a company renowned and respected throughout central Scotland, but virtually unknown beyond that limited sphere. In less than a decade it had been transformed into a national force truly to be reckoned with.

Her eyes drifted to his free hand that still held the paper-knife, to the clever, manipulative fingers that toyed idly with the blade. His dynamic progress had never surprised her. Since those days when he had been a minor editorial manager and she an awestruck trainee sub, she had known the restless energy that burned within him. It was what had drawn her to him. She still felt its pull.

But in those early days it had lacked a focus and had been dissipated unproductively in rugby and fast cars—not to mention also in his brief pursuit of her. That day his elder brother, Niall, had been killed, thrusting Rory, at first reluctantly, into the boardroom to take his place, the lives of many had been changed forever.

For that had been the end and the beginning. The end of the old order and the beginning of the new. And he had soon enough made it painfully clear to her to which of these two orders she belonged.

Almost unconsciously now her eyes dropped down to the desk-top, scanning its surface on a pretext of idle interest, though she knew exactly what she was looking for. And there it was, its back towards her, a silver-framed photograph propped decorously in one corner. He was now bound, it appeared, by all regular conventions. He even had a photograph of his wife on his desk!

As she averted her eyes, she felt a stab of self-pity. It seemed pretty well certain that no photo of herself was ever destined to grace any man's desk, in spite of all the hopes she had so recently nurtured. She crushed the thought from her. It was weak and broody. She had come home to forget, not to dwell on such things.

He had finished speaking and was laying the phone down, leaning back in his leather swivel chair with the paper-knife balanced like a steely suspension bridge between the index fingers of his two hands. The tawny eyes regarded her over the top of it.

'So, where were we? Ah, yes. You were listing my misdemeanours.' His tone was supremely unperturbed. Clearly he cared nothing for her displeasure. 'Do you wish to continue, or shall we move on to a fresh subject? That one, I confess, has limited appeal.'

He smiled a smile that might have melted her soul, had it not, irredeemably, been frozen against him. 'Why not let's talk about you for a change? It's been so long. What have you been up to?'

Isla leaned back a little in her chair and fought back the stirrings of irritation and resentment. What she had been 'up to' for the past eight years had been the process of restructuring a shattered life, starting again from the very beginning. That she had succeeded was the source of her strength and self-esteem. She had made something of her life in spite of him.

She looked across at him now through hostile violet eyes. 'I haven't come here to discuss my business. I've explained already what I've come for.' She paused to slice him a look of censure. 'I want your guarantee that you'll shelve your plans to build on that land in front of my parents' cottage.'

With a flick of his wrist and impeccable timing, and without for one fraction of a second detaching his dark tawny eyes from Isla's, Rory spun the paper-knife into the air and caught it deftly by its handle. 'They tell me you're a big shot down in London. The high-powered editor of a fashion magazine. Not bad for a little country girl from Strathallane.'

Isla smiled without humour at his blatant condescension and returned to the question he had so cleverly ignored. 'Do I have your guarantee or not? To obtain that guarantee is the only reason I've come here.'

'Mind you, I always knew you had it in you.' He continued as though she had never spoken. '*Chloe*—that's the magazine you're in charge of, isn't it? It's a leader in its field, by all accounts.'

Isla felt like picking up one of the phones and smashing it over his obdurate head. With an effort of will she fought back the impulse and resigned herself to going along with him for a bit. The alternative, she sensed, was an endless verbal ping pong, with each of them playing their own separate balls. 'I left *Chloe* several months ago,' she informed him in a cool tone. 'After four years as its editor, I felt I needed a new challenge. For the past few months I've been working on the pilot issue of a new magazine, still within the same company.'

'Good for you. What sort of magazine is it?'

'Similar to *Chloe*, but for a slightly older market. Less fashion and beauty, more general features.'

What she was telling him was true, but it was also a lie, for she was omitting one crucial piece of information. Plans to launch the new magazine had been dropped just two weeks ago, leaving her, essentially, out of a job.

Not that that in itself represented a problem. She'd already had several very tempting offers. The problem was deciding which one to go for, a task which was proving impossibly difficult—and just another of the hornet's nest of reasons that had persuaded her to spend some time north of the border. The peace and quiet of Strathallane, she had hoped, might be more conducive to the making of vital decisions than the frantic hurly-burly of London.

If she had suspected for one moment that her flight to Strathallane would result in her getting mixed up with Rory Buchanan, her holiday plans would have been very different.

She could tell he was about to ask another question and they had already dwelt quite long enough on the subject of her. If he continued to probe, she might well end up in a discussion about her professional future. And her professional future and everything else about her were no longer any concern of Rory Buchanan's.

She held up her hand. 'Look, I know you're a busy man and I'm sure you have better things to do than sit here chatting. Can't you just give me the guarantee I'm asking for? Then I'll be on my way and I won't bother you again.'

As an offer it was the very essence of reasonableness. One might have expected it to provoke a reasonable response. Or rather, one might conceivably have expected such a thing had one been dealing with a man other than Rory Buchanan.

A pair of golden eagle eyes regarded her unblinkingly across the desk-top. 'And why should I give you such a guarantee? The land is mine to do with as I please.'

Isla's heart sank. 'But surely you don't need it! Whatever it is you're planning to build there, you could build on another piece of land elsewhere. Somewhere where it wouldn't matter. There must be dozens of other sites you could use!'

'But why should I look for another site when I already have one that suits my purposes perfectly?'

'So you do intend to build?'

He did not answer. He did not have to. A look of pure arrogance shone from his eyes.

'What have you got in mind? Some factory? Some plant? Maybe even some multi-storey eyesore of an office block?' Suddenly she was beside herself with fury. She sprang to her feet, her eyes flashing her anger at him. 'Well, don't think I plan to stand by and let you get away with it. I'm not one of your brow-beaten local chattels who let you walk all over them, just because of your name! I'm not afraid of you, Rory Buchanan! And I'm damned if I'll let you get away with this!'

For a moment he just sat and stared at her, his eyes as hard as lumps of topaz. Then with a gesture of impatience he tossed aside the paper-knife, so that it skittered violently over the desk-top. 'So, you've come up here thinking to lay down the law?' The words lunged at her like an unsheathed sword. She felt them whip dangerously close to her face. Then with a sudden brusque movement he, too, was on his feet, coming round the desk to stand before her. 'Perhaps you're used to throwing your weight around down in London, but I wouldn't try it here, if I were you!'

Isla had forgotten how tall he was, how broad his shoulders, how strong his physique. She had forgotten, too, the sheer electric power he seemed to exert over her at close proximity. It entered her now and flooded through her, overwhelming her utterly, fixing her to the spot.

'Why don't you go back to London and mind your own damned business?' He was growling the words down at her through angrily bared teeth.

'What goes on up here has nothing to do with you. You have no place up here any more!'

The arrogance of the accusation shook her back to life. Glaring at him, she took a stumbling step away. 'And since when did *you* decide who belongs and who doesn't? Have you all of a sudden become the law around here?' She stood back on the heels of her navy calfskin boots and glared at him with outrage and dislike. 'It's time someone took you down a peg or two. You're too damned important for your own good!'

'Is that a fact?' he taunted her, taking a threatening step towards her. 'And since when did you ever give a damn about anyone else's good but your own?' He narrowed his eyes at her, his expression dark and poisonous. 'I'm sure life in the big city suits you perfectly. There you can pursue your selfish little existence among millions of faceless others just like yourself.' With a contemptuous gesture he swung away, then, a few feet away, turned once more to face her. 'Do us all a favour and take my advice. Get out of here and go back where you belong.'

'Not until I'm good and ready!' All at once Isla's heart was beating briskly. The personal tenor of his attack had surprised and shaken her and left her feeling slightly bewildered, quite at a loss to know what had provoked it. It had succeeded in touching an unexpected raw spot.

With a monumental effort she clung on to her composure and struggled to stop her limbs from trembling. 'I'll leave as soon as I decide to leave!' she flung back at him. 'And you can take my word for it that that won't be until I'm sure that nothing is going to be built on that land. Either you can give that assurance voluntarily, or I shall be forced to take certain measures against you!'

'So, you're looking for a fight?' Rory's tawny eyes raked her. Belligerently, he thrust back the sides of his jacket and faced her full square, hands on hips. 'If that's what you're after, I won't disappoint you. I'll damn well give you the fight of your life!'

He stood like a quivering Colossus over her, his anger so real she could have reached out and touched it. Thrusting back her shoulders, Isla straightened perceptibly and glared violet daggers into his eyes. 'As it happens, I didn't come looking for a fight. I thought we might be able to reach some amicable agreement——'

'Then you wasted your time,' Rory cut in rudely before she had the chance to go on to assure him that, if it came to a fight, she would not shrink from it either. Immune to her daggers, he continued, 'The day I take orders from the likes of you will be the day that rivers run upstream. My advice to you is, don't hold your breath. Just get on the first train back to London.'

'I think you misheard me.' Isla's tone was sharp. Never had she felt such anger seething through her. 'I said I had no intention of leaving until I'd put a stop to these plans of yours.' On legs stiff with fury she swung away. 'You'll be hearing from my parents' solicitor!'

'You're wasting your time.' His taunts followed her to the door. 'You can take whatever measures you please, but I can promise you you're not going to change a damned thing!'

Isla paused for a moment with her hand on the door-handle. 'We'll see about that!' she flung back over her shoulder. 'You may just be in for a nasty surprise!'

Then she was striding out into the outer office, past the wide-eyed secretary towards the lift. A nasty surprise was indeed what awaited him if he believed that he could trample all over her again, as he had done so cruelly once before!

Down on the ground floor she walked smartly past Reception and headed for the main door, without a glance left or right. He had said he would give her the fight of her life. Likewise, she would give him the fight of his. And, what was more, she would emerge the victor.

She turned up the collar of her navy cashmere coat and stepped out into a thickening flurry of snowflakes. And suddenly the sense of resolve in her heart was as cold and unrelenting as the bitter December wind.

CHAPTER TWO

ISLA'S quivering anger sustained her throughout the drive back to her parents' cottage. Her knuckles were white as she gripped the steering-wheel, her jaw fiercely clenched from the fury within her.

She had known that the meeting with Rory would be difficult. Only a sense of duty towards her parents had persuaded her that she must go through with it, and, even then, she had proceeded with the greatest reluctance. After all, for eight whole years she had avoided all contact with the man. On her sporadic visits north of the border she had painstakingly gone out of her way to avoid him. If the truth were known it had been her greatest desire that she might never set eyes on him again.

But what choice had she had when faced with the dilemma that her parents currently found themselves in? Her mother had literally been in floods of tears while recounting the tragedy that was soon to befall them.

'We thought we'd escaped when old Jock Campbell died and left that piece of land to his nephew in Brisbane. We thought it would just be left as it was and that we didn't have to worry about it any more.'

As she had dabbed at her cheeks with a bedraggled pink tissue, Isla had laid a comforting hand on her arm and silently run over in her mind the long-running saga of Jock Campbell's field.

The field, which flanked the MacDonalds' front garden, had lain idle for many years, inhabited only sporadically by a pair of donkeys primed with the task of keeping the weeds under control. Then had come the news, about three or four years ago, that Jock was planning to build a couple of bungalows on the land.

Quite understandably, this news had struck panic in the MacDonalds' hearts. The field was less than an acre in all. By necessity the bungalows would be cheek by jowl with the MacDonalds' little cottage, entirely putting an end to their privacy and—even worse—blocking their magnificent view. For their principal reason for buying the cottage had been in order that they might enjoy the breathtaking panoramas it afforded northwards over the Grampian Mountains, the glorious foothills of the Highlands. The prospect before them, literally, had been devastating.

Protests had been made and petitions drawn up— for they had not been alone in their horror at these plans—but all, alas, to no avail. Jock Campbell had been granted planning permission and building had been scheduled to begin in the spring.

But then, as though by divine intervention, the eighty-year-old Jock had upped and died, leaving his estate to a scattering of offspring and the field specifically to a nephew in Australia. As the plans for the bungalows were suspended the MacDonalds had breathed a sigh of relief.

For two blissful years nothing had happened, and then, just a couple of months ago, word had gone round that the land was up for auction. A week or so later it had gone down to the highest bidder, a company by the name of Cairngorm Holdings.

'We don't know who they are,' Isobel MacDonald had wailed to her daughter. 'Only that they're land and property developers. It looks as though we're right back where we started.'

It had taken Isla just a moment for the news to sink in. Cairngorm Holdings ... The name rang a bell. And then, like a blue flash bursting in her head, suddenly, it had come to her. 'I know who Cairngorm Holdings belongs to! It's one of Buchanan's minor subsidiaries!' Not for nothing had she over the years made a point of keeping up to date with the progress of the company of her ex-lover.

'Buchanan's? Are you sure?' Her mother had blinked at her.

'Yes, I'm sure,' Isla had nodded, already guessing with a sense of dread at the favour her mother was about to ask of her.

'Oh, Isla, would you speak to Rory for us? I know it's a long time since you two were friends, but I'm sure you could handle it better than your father and I. Besides,' she had added, twisting her fingers, 'your father's not able for such things at the moment. The doctors have told him he must avoid all stress. It would only do him harm if he were to involve himself in this.'

What could she do? She could hardly say no. So she had nodded and patted her mother's hand. 'OK, I'll do what I can,' she had promised. 'I'll go and speak to him tomorrow.'

It seemed such a small thing to do for her parents, but she would sooner have locked horns with the devil himself.

Now, as she drove her parents' Renault through the cloud-capped, snow-sprinkled Vale of Strathallane, she was immune to the silent splendour all around her. All she knew was the anger that possessed her and the violent turmoil of her heart. Damn you to infinity, Rory Buchanan! she railed at him silently beneath her breath. Damn you for ever having walked into my live—and myself for allowing you back into it again!

It was hard to remember she had not always felt that way. Once, her feelings had been very different.

She had gone to work for Buchanan's straight from school, a proud, excited, innocent seventeen-year-old with dreams of a journalistic career. Assigned to *Juliet*, a weekly for women, as a humble trainee sub-editor, secretly she had nutured ambitions of one day becoming its editor. Little had she guessed at how painfully short her career at Buchanan's was destined to be. And even less could she have guessed at the cause of her departure.

For in under a year her entire world would be turned upside-down and inside-out when, with bitter and tragically far-reaching consequences, she was to fall hopelessly in love with the boss's son.

At that time Rory was the misfit, the rebel, a young man who seemed to be going nowhere. The second son of Duncan Buchanan, who still ran the company virtually single-handedly, he showed no great interest in his father's business, preferring to spend his time hell-raising and racing cars. Meanwhile, being primed as Duncan's eventual successor was Rory's elder brother, the level-headed Niall, as different from Rory as velvet from rough linen, yet adored for all that by his wayward sibling.

The meeting between the wide-eyed, unworldly Isla and the irrepressible, devil-may-care Rory had been one of those cruel accidents of fate. On one of Rory's rare visits to Buchanan's they had been caught alone together in a lift that got stuck. Twenty minutes later, when they were finally released, Isla knew that she was well and truly smitten. They had been the funniest, most entertaining—and most breathlessly exciting—twenty minutes of her life. And when Rory started hanging around the *Juliet* offices, it looked as though, possibly, he was smitten too.

They had started going out together. Parties, cinemas, sailing, riding. No two dates were ever the same. With Rory, Isla to her delight was discovering, life was a never-ending adventure. The only thing she could ever be sure of was that, like a conjurer, he would always surprise her.

And yet, beneath that torrent of boundless energy that he seemed to scatter indiscriminately in all directions, at times she could sense a deeper core of purpose. A crystal-hard kernel of ambition that would provide the foundations of the man he was to become. That Sunday afternoon up on Ben Vorlich was possibly the first time she had glimpsed it.

They had spread a blanket on the heather for a picnic and were polishing off a pizza and a bottle of white wine when Rory had reached across and slipped an arm around her shoulder.

'One day all of that could be yours,' he told her, waving his free hand at the hills and valleys that stretched out endlessly before them. He turned to look at her, his tawny eyes serious. 'But only if you stick with me.'

Isla had felt an almost painful jolt within her. It was not the first time in their short but intense relationship that he had made allusions to a possible future together. And, aware of how much she longed for that to happen, she could not help but fear that he might only be joking. So she had deliberately skirted round that loaded issue and concentrated on the rest of his remark.

'I didn't know Buchanan's owned all of Tayside!' she'd joked, smiling back at him through violet eyes. 'Perhaps this is something you ought to tell me about!'

Rory had leaned back against the blanket, drawing her down with him into his arms. 'It doesn't belong to Buchanan's, but it's going to be mine. And I didn't mean Tayside, I meant the world. All of it, further than the eye can see.' He dropped his head back and gazed into the sky, then turned to look at her again, a strange new intensity shining in his eyes. 'Do you believe me, Isla?' he'd asked her. 'Do you think that I can do it?'

To be perfectly honest, at that moment, Isla hadn't really understood what he was saying. Yet as she'd looked into his face with its clear bright eyes, straight black brows and firm, strong jaw, she had known that, whatever his dream might be, without a doubt he would achieve it. She had nodded. 'Of course I think you can do it. I think you can do anything you choose.'

He had smiled then, that smile that could melt her bones, and leaned to cover her mouth with his. 'You're the only one who believes in me. If you want me to, I'll take you with me,' he'd promised.

'Oh, I want to, I want to,' she had murmured beneath her breath, as his arms had drawn her even closer. No prize that heaven or earth could offer could have seemed to her even half as wonderful as the promise of a lifetime with this wild, wonderful man who stirred her soul and lit up her senses.

Over the months the promises had grown more specific. 'One day we'll be married,' he'd told her often. And though he had never suggested a formal engagement, that had not bothered Isla unduly. Rory was not the kind to observe such formalities. What mattered was what he had decided in his heart.

It was on her eighteenth birthday that they had first made love.

It had not been planned, but before the evening had even begun both of them had known it was destined to happen. Rory had borrowed the flat of a friend and arranged a lavish party for her, and at the party's climax he had given her a gold bracelet, bearing one simple charm, a solid gold heart.

'Every year on your birthday I'll give you another one,' he'd told her, holding her to him and kissing her warmly. 'And I promise there'll be an extra special one on the day that we get married.'

It had been a magical evening that neither had wanted to end, but the crowd, the noise, in the end had overwhelmed them and they had had to escape to be alone for a while. They had driven to a spot by the banks of Loch Lomond, a favourite spot that they often went to, and there, beneath an August moon, as they lay stretched on the cool, soft grassy bank listening to the ripple of the water, inevitably, one thing had led to another.

'I love you, my sweet Isla,' he had whispered to her, as his fingers had fumbled with the fastening of her dress. And, as it had slipped from her shoulders, a shudder had gone through her.

'I could never love anyone as I love you.'

He had buried his face against her naked breasts, caressing her, loving her, his breath thick with emotion. And she had driven her fingers through his thick dark hair, longing for him, adoring him, yet deeply apprehensive amid the spiralling excitement she had felt. For even then she had known deep in her heart that she was on the brink of something so enormous that it must eventually either redeem or devastate her life.

After that first blissful, bittersweet joining, they made love hungrily, secretly, again and again. And to Isla it had seemed as though her entire being, body and soul, were being fused to his. There could be no life without Rory. No laughter, no meaning. He was her present, her future, her dreams. Her everything.

And that knowledge gave birth to a dreadful fear. For what if she should ever lose him?

It had been around that time that, out of the blue, Donald Buchanan, Rory's father, had died. Fifty-two years old, the victim of a stroke. The Buchanans and Strathallane had been devastated. But worse, much worse, was still to come. Less than two months after Donald's death, Niall, his heir, was killed in a flying accident. The entire community went into a state of shock.

The awful weeks and months that followed were branded indelibly on Isla's brain. In the face of Rory's terrible grief she had felt shut out, afraid, impotent and useless. The bond that had grown between them seemed fractured and sterile. In the darkness of his sorrow he had seemed to slip away from her. And all her deepest fears seemed about to be realised.

Bewildered and terrified of making a wrong move, she had kept her distance in those early days. Once he had come to terms with his devastating loss things between them would return to normal. At least, that was what she had hoped and prayed for, but it had soon become clear, in spite of her prayers, that nothing would ever be the same again.

For one thing, Rory had undergone a metamorphosis. Thrust as he was without warning and no preparation into a position of power and responsibility, his previous feckless image seemed to have dropped away from him like the chrysalis skin of a newly emerged butterfly. Overnight he had become the lonely head of a company whose inner workings he knew virtually nothing about, and his need to learn and master his new role was a need with which he had seemed obsessed. All at once he had had little time for anything else, and virtually no time at all for Isla.

The promises of marriage had never been withdrawn, but, notably, neither had they been repeated. With subtle hints, by closing her out, he had seemed to be trying to tell her it was over. She had belonged to his previous life. It had seemed she had no place in this new one.

Isla had been possessed of too much pride to beg or even to insist that he clarify the situation. She had accepted the hints and with pain in her heart had taken it upon herself to cut the ties finally.

A colleague, recently moved to London to work on a well-known magazine there, had written to tell Isla that there was another vacancy. Grabbing at the chance to salvage her integrity, Isla applied and got the job. And all that Rory had said when she had told him was, 'Congratulations. I wish you luck.'

Now, as she turned off the main road by the wood and headed for her parents' cottage, her fingers were tight around the steering-wheel of the Renault. No one had known what it had cost her to leave then. No one had known of the secret she had carried. And no one, she was determined, would ever know of the secret wounds that had scarred her forever.

She came round the bend and caught sight of the cottage, the little stone cottage where she had been born and raised. When she had left, in her heart, she had known it would be forever, although she had prayed that Rory would come after her and bring her back.

Needless to say, no such thing had happened and it had been two months before she had set eyes on him again. Passing through London, he had dropped by to visit her. 'For old times' sake.' She remembered his words. But, by then, even if he had begged her on his knees to return, nothing could have dragged her back to Strathallane. Nor could she ever have found it in her heart to forgive him for what he had done to her.

Too much had happened. There had been too much suffering. And the love in her heart had turned to hate.

She swung off the road and through the narrow gates to the cottage. Then, as she pulled on the handbrake, she glanced across her shoulder at the still-empty field beyond the wooden fencing, letting her gaze rise upwards to the mountains beyond. And as her eyes scanned their familiar snow-capped beauty, she felt a surge of strengthening resolve within her. Rory Buchanan had done enough damage to one MacDonald already. He would not get away with this latest threat to her parents.

With a firming of her jaw, she climbed out of the car and allowed herself a wry fleeting smile. In a way it was really almost pleasurable to have so clear a focus for her anger against him. After all those years she could at last give vent to all the hurt and resentment that had built up inside her.

She headed for the cottage with a spring in her step. She was going to enjoy the battle ahead.

Isla's visit to the solicitor was not encouraging.

'We've alredy explored all the avenues open to us, Miss MacDonald,' he explained with a regretful shake of his head. 'I don't in all honesty think there are any legal means left to us to prevent Mr Buchanan from building on that land whenever he chooses.'

'Isn't there even some way to stop him temporarily? Just long enough to give us some time to maybe come up with some solution we haven't thought of?'

'Not unless the plans he submits contravene the terms set out in the planning agreement. That's really the only hope we have.'

And that amounted to no hope at all, Isla acknowledged to herself with a sense of frustration as she finally left the solicitor's office and stepped out into the busy pre-Christmas street. Rory Buchanan would not make an elementary mistake like that. Whatever else he was, he was a damn shrewd operator.

Which left her with something of a dilemma. Where on earth did she go from here? Apart from her own personal interest in the matter, her parents were relying on her to handle it for them. If she failed them, they would have no one else to turn to. With her older sister married to a Dutchman and living in Antwerp for the past ten years, she, Isla, was effectively the only one they had to turn to. It would be unforgivable if she were to let them down.

She pulled up the collar of her navy cashmere coat as, brow furrowed, she strode down the windy street. She wasn't beaten yet. She would think of something. She had to. It was a matter of honour.

And then, just as she was about to cross the road to the car park, he suddenly appeared at the end of the street. A tall dark figure in a black wool overcoat, laden with parcels, striding in her direction.

He had not spotted her, of that she was certain, and Isla's first instinct was to dive into a doorway and hide until he had gone past. That was what she would have done in the past. Anything in the world to avoid him.

But, instead, she remained exactly where she was, only a touch of apprehension flickering through her as her eyes searched among the crowd of Christmas shoppers for the face of Evelyn—Evelyn, his wife. But as his tall figure came closer, parting the crowd effortlessly, she could see that he was quite alone. More than likely, she thought, eyeing his parcels, he had been out doing a bit of last-minute Christmas shopping.

He caught sight of her at the very last moment. His attention, it appeared, had been miles away. And she could see from the expression that flitted across his face, darkening his features and drawing together the black brows, that his initial reaction, similar to her own, had been, quite simply, to walk on by. This intention she instantly defeated by very deliberately stepping in front of him.

'Surely you weren't thinking of passing an old friend without even pausing to say hello?'

The tawny eyes looked down at her, as sharp as an eagle's. He smiled briefly and harshly. 'Hello, Isla,' he conceded. Then immediately he made as though to move on past her, precisely as he had initially intended.

Isla shifted to block him. 'You're in a hurry. Don't you even have time for a friendly chat?'

A look of pained resignation settled on his face, although the lines around his mouth and his jaw were still hard. 'What is it you want? You'd better come out with it. I don't have time to waste on friendly chats, as you call them.'

Close to, in the cold December light, his features seemed almost carved from stone. The slightly crooked nose that lent his features their harsh pride, the broad, intelligent planes of his brow, the high, taut cheekbones, the quarrelsome chin. Even the mouth that could smile with such heart-stopping sweetness and convey through its kisses a strength of passion that could rip to shreds an unwary soul, at this moment was drawn in a firm, hard line. Beneath the straight black brows the tawny eyes glittered with all the warmth and compassion of an Arctic ice flow.

He was wearing a dark wool suit beneath the dark overcoat. Layer upon layer of darkness, Isla pondered. A darkness that went right through to his soul. Eight years ago she had seen only his light side. But then eight years ago she had been a fool.

Sarcastically, she demanded, 'What's the hurry? Are you so keen to get home to wrap up your parcels?'

'Something like that.' His gaze never wavered. 'But you haven't answered my question yet. Why are you bothering me? What do you want?'

So, he found her a bother? That was some satisfaction. It appeared she was starting to get under his skin. 'I think you know what I want of you,' she answered. 'I spelled it out to you quite clearly in your office yesterday.'

The tawny eyes narrowed. 'Spell it out again. I fear it may just have slipped my mind.'

She ignored the biting sarcasm and looked straight at him, raising in challenge one perfectly pencilled eyebrow. 'Since your memory appears to be so unreliable, let me refresh it for you in words of one syllable. What I want of you is your guarantee that you will drop all plans to build on that land. And in case you've also forgotten what land we happen to be talking about, the land in question is old Jock Campbell's field.'

Rory raised one of his own dark eyebrows and met her challenge without a flicker. 'I fear it's *your* memory, not mine that's unreliable. As I recall, I have already given you my answer. I am not, repeat *not*, in the habit of giving such guarantees to anyone. What I choose to do on my land is my business. I, most certainly, am not accountable to you.'

Isla felt the dam of her anger burst within her. She was trembling with frustration as she demanded, 'Does that mean you plan to go ahead?'

'Affirmative.' He lanced her a look of impatience. 'Surely you didn't really believe I would be prepared to change my plans for you?'

'But you have no right to do what you're intending! It's not fair! It's not decent! Surely you know that!' As, with a dismissive gesture, he made to move past her, she stumbled in front of him again and grabbed him by the arm. 'No one with any decency could even think of doing what you're doing!'

As she continued to stand belligerently before him, blocking his path on the crowded pavement, she was aware of a rising pulse of dark energy within him. Every sinew, every nerve-end of his powerful body seemed to shimmer with an anger barely held in check. With frozen features he lowered his eyes pointedly to her hand that still clutched at the sleeve of his coat. 'I've said what I have to say. Now do you intend releasing me—or would you prefer to have a scene right here in the street?'

The cold disdain on his face was shocking, and it was that somehow more than his refusal to co-operate that seemed to tip the balance of Isla's composure. 'Is that what you're afraid of? A scene in the street?' As she raised her voice in shrill demand, she was aware of one or two passers-by glancing curiously across at them. That would nor-mally have stopped her in her tracks—public scenes were something she abhorred—but at that moment, on the windswept high street of Strathallane, some inner madness had taken hold of her.

'I suppose it wouldn't look too good for a local big shot like yourself to be seen brawling in the street with an ex-girlfriend! What would people think? And what about your wife? What would she have to say if she got to hear about it?' The words came out in an unstoppable shrill stream, as though she had no power to control them. She tore at his sleeve with furious fingers. 'Your precious position as head of Buchanan's and your damned marriage of convenience, that's all you care about!'

The next insant, roughly, he had snatched his arm away, and in the very same movement grabbed her by the wrist. His fingers closed around her delicate tendons like a band of vicious, unrelenting steel. He snatched her to him, his face like thunder.

'Don't push me, Isla. You'll only be sorry.' His tone was dangerous, low and menacing. His eyes drove into her like skewers. 'I've told you once before and I'll tell you once again, you've made a very big mistake if you think that you can come up here and start throwing your weight around. Take my advice. Go back where you came from.' Abruptly, he released her. 'Go back and stay there!'

For one vivid moment he remained standing over her, dark and chilling in his terrible anger. And as Isla looked up at him all she could think of, with a sense of bewildered desolation, was that nothing and no one ever before had caused her to lose control like that. All her carefully nurtured poise, in one instant of madness, had blown up in her face.

Still trembling and shaky, she took a step back as, like a whirlwind, he went sweeping past her. Then helplessly she watched as, like some prince of darkness, the black coat billowing out behind him, he went striding off into the crowd.

CHAPTER THREE

THE next couple of days were blessedly peaceful.
Isla spent them at home with her parents, pottering
about in the kitchen with her mother, helping her
with the Christmas preparations, or sitting round
the log fire, chatting with her father. It was precisely the sort of relaxation she was in need of. She
could feel her inner batteries recharging.

Fortunately there had been no more encounters
with Rory, for which small blessing she felt endlessly thankful. That last encounter with him in the
high street when her self-control had collapsed like
a deck-chair had left her feeling badly shaken. It
just wasn't like her to behave that way, shrieking
like a fishwife in a public street and making a
shameful spectacle of herself. It was the sort of
behaviour she abhorred and despised.

And the things she had said! she had thought
later, cringing. What madness on earth had
possessed her? All that vitriolic stuff about his
marriage of convenience and what his wife would
think if she could see them. It was as though all
the pent-up resentments of eight years had come
pouring out in an unstoppable stream. She blanched
now to think that she had really said it. She would
have given her right arm if it could only be *un*said.

For it had all been just a little too revealing, just
a little too close to the bone. That she had never
forgiven Rory for marrying Evelyn just two years

after her own flight to London was something she preferred to keep to herself.

There was no need at all for the world to know that the news of the marriage had broken her heart, her poor battered heart that had barely been healed.

Of course, she had understood the reason for the marriage. As the only remaining male Buchanan, Rory needed a wife to give him heirs, and Evelyn McDiarmid, the eligible daughter of a wealthy local industrial family, was a wife of whom Rory's mother would approve. But, understanding aside, Isla had hated him for it. In her eyes it had merely been another demonstration of how very little she had ever really meant to him.

It had been some consolation that in six years of marriage no heir, in fact, had been produced, for Isla knew that when that eventually happened it would be the greatest grief she would ever have to bear. For six years her almost obsessive dread of it had fuelled her hatred and fed her resentment.

But her own private agonies were not for public consumption and she would never forgive herself for that terrible scene. Yet it had served one purpose in that it had warned her of how deeply he was still capable of affecting her. From now on she must keep a tight grip on her self-control.

For now, however, she was planning a few days' respite. Then once Christmas was past she would consider very carefully what her next move ought to be.

In the meantime, she was enjoying being back in Strathallane and having time to spend with her parents. 'We don't see nearly enough of you, Isla,' her mother chided gently on Christmas Eve afternoon as they beavered away together in the cosy little kitchen, preparing a special trifle for next day's dinner. 'I know we're a long way away from London, but your father and I really miss you, my dear. Still, we understand.' She smiled at her daughter. 'We know how busy that job of yours keeps you. It's a very important position you have.'

Isla paused in arranging her slices of sponge cake over the bottom of the crystal dessert dish and reached out to squeeze her mother's arm. 'Non-sense,' she protested. 'There's nothing important about it. And, anyway,' she reminded her mother with a giggle, 'I happen to be jobless at the moment!'

'You won't be for long,' her mother insisted. 'You'll soon be moving on to even better things. Your father and I have no doubts about that.'

Isla smiled at her, pleased by the pride in her voice and grateful for the faith her parents had always shown in her. Yet at that moment she felt a million miles removed from the high-powered executive image of herself. Standing there now in a shapeless old sweater and a pair of well-worn baggy jeans, with not a scrap of make-up adorning her face and her chestnut bob decidedly dishev-elled, she felt almost like a different person. And it was a lovely feeling, she reflected happily. One she would dearly like to feel more often.

She offered a smile as she assured her mother, 'I'm sorry I don't see you as often as I ought to. I'll try to do better in the future.'

How she was going to manage it she had no idea, but she suddenly did feel truly ashamed of the way she had been neglecting her parents. After all, they weren't getting any younger and an annual flying three-day visit at Christmas, which was all she had managed over the past three years, really was not good enough.

She frowned inwardly as she thought for the first time in days of the three job offers she had to choose from, two in London and one in America. Mentally now she discarded that last one. In view of the promise she had just made to her mother, it wasn't really feasible.

The sudden decision instantly warmed her. Perhaps things were starting to fall into place.

'I just remembered. I didn't show you this.' Mrs MacDonald laid aside her bowl of whipping cream, wiped her hands on a tea-towel and reached into her apron pocket. Beaming proudly, she pulled out a snapshot. 'It came with Heather's card this morning.'

'Oh, let me see it!' With a surge of pleasure Isla reached out and took the snapshot from her mother. Then she smiled as she looked down at the photo of her older sister arm in arm with her seven-year-old daughter, Rebecca. 'What a beautiful little girl she's growing up to be. And she's a real MacDonald. Just look at that hair!' Yet her genuine delight was oddly mingled with a secret, poignant sense of regret. Would that Rebecca had been her own child, the daughter she had never had.

She stifled the thought and composed herself swiftly as she handed the snapshot back to her mother. 'Heather's looking well as usual,' she remarked warmly, as she emptied a can of pears over the carefully arranged sponge slices. 'The life of a Dutch businessman's wife seems to suit her.'

'Pieter's a good man. That's why she's happy.' As Mrs MacDonald slid the snapshot back into her pocket, she cast a sideways glance at her younger daughter, and Isla knew exactly what was coming next. She shook her head and smiled as her mother continued, 'I wish I could see you happily settled, too. This career of yours is all very well, but when are you going to find yourself a good man?'

As always, Isla parried by making a joke out of it. 'Good men are hard to find these days. Heather and her kind seem to have snapped them all up.'

'Good men have always been hard to find—but I found myself one and so did your sister.' Mrs MacDonald observed her with a canny eye. 'What happened to that James chap you wrote to us about?'

Isla felt the faintest clench in her stomach. The subject of James was one she had been hoping to avoid. 'I'm afraid he turned out to be anything but a good man. I discovered a little while back that he was married.'

'Married?' Her mother's eyes widened in horror. Isla could sense that her heart-rate had probably doubled. In Strathallane girls who fooled around with married men were very definitely disapproved of.

'Don't worry,' Isla assured her, pursing her lips wryly, as she reflected that it was not a pastime she approved of much either. 'I found out in plenty of time. Long before things got out of hand.' She met her mother's eyes to ensure that she had understood fully. 'And, of course, the minute I found out I dropped him.'

Her mother's anxious expression softened as she turned her attention back to the trifle. 'Oh, Isla,' she muttered with a heartfelt sigh. 'You just don't seem to have any luck with men at all.'

Never had a truer word been spoken, Isla had no choice but to acknowledge to herself. Love was a prize that consistently eluded her. She never even seemed to come anywhere near.

She had had high hopes of James at the beginning. It had seemed as though he might be just what she was looking for. For, although many of her friends and colleagues down in London had her figured as a career woman with no interest in marriage, in her heart she nurtured the fervent dream that one day she would find a man with whom to share her life.

But each and every one of her romantic forays had inevitably turned into a resounding disaster. Her love-life was nothing but a series of false starts. Men who turned out to be secretly pining for another, confirmed bachelors or men who were married to their work. And now this latest disappointment, a man who already had a flesh-and-blood wife.

It had been partly to help her recover from this latest romantic fiasco that Isla had decided to spend some time with her parents. It was not that she had been deeply in love with James, nor that the ending of their relationship had been in any way devastating. But it had hurt all the same, it had been yet another let-down, and it had made her wonder where she was going wrong.

'Perhaps I ought to resign myself to being an old maid forever,' she suggested to her mother, only half joking. 'Perhaps my Mr Right just doesn't exist.'

Her mother eyed her wisely. 'Nonsense, my girl. You're just looking for him in all the wrong places.' Then she finished piping the whipped cream with a flourish. 'There now! What do you think of that?'

All the cooking that could be done had been done, the tree had been decorated and the presents were all wrapped when Isla and her parents set out later that night to attend the watch-night service at the local kirk.

The snow that had been falling on and off all day was coming down now in a thick, steady swirl, dancing in the headlights of the Renault as they made their way along the narrow country lanes to the ivy-covered greystone church.

Isla sat in the front seat next to her father, squinting out at the snow-softened landscape and feeling peculiarly content to be back here again. It was all so tranquil and reassuring, just as it had been throughout her childhood, with a totally dependable, enduring quality that was soothing to her troubled mind. At times, in her teens, she had rejected that quality and longed instead for what was new and different. Now she found it immensely reassuring that, although people might change, Strathallane remained the same.

She smiled to herself. I must be getting old to find myself so seduced by all this peace and tranquillity. But I don't care, she decided, sitting back in her seat and turning up the collar of her navy cashmere coat. For the moment it's exactly what I need. A couple of weeks will pass quickly enough and I'll be back in the roar and the rush of London before I even know it's gone.

At the thought a brief scurry of anxiety went through her, a reaction that surprised and slightly alarmed her. In the past the thought of returning to her life in London had always filled her with excitement.

It's just because of all the question marks I have hanging over my head, she decided quickly, rationalising her uneasiness. After all, I still have to decide about my career. I can't put off that decision forever.

But impatiently she pushed these thoughts away. Time enough to think about all that in a couple of days' time when all the Christmas celebrations were over. For the moment, as she had already solemnly promised herself, at least until after Boxing Day, she would allow nothing and nobody with the power to upset her even to enter into her head.

And that included Rory Buchanan and his plans to build in Jock Campbell's field. For the next couple of days she refused even to think about it. After all, with Christmas upon them, there was nothing to be done. Rory would be far too busy with his family even to give the matter a second thought.

They came round the bend on to the narrow church road and at the sight of the familiar floodlit building, its narrow grey spire reaching up into the sky while all around the snowflakes swirled and spun, an unexpected lump rose in Isla's throat.

This was the same little church she had attended as a child, the church where Heather and Pieter had been married. It looked so small and picturesque, like a picture postcard painting amid the tall, snow-laden trees, and yet at the same time so solid, so substantial. It had served the local faithful for three hundred years. It would continue to serve them for three hundred more.

A little throng of people were filing into the church, smiling and murmuring greetings to one another. Isla followed her parents into the simple interior with its Christmas tree beneath the pulpit and took her seat beside them in the MacDonald family pew while the organist played a medley of Christmas carols.

The whole scene brought back memories of a dozen childhood Christmases. She smiled at her mother. 'I'm so glad we came.'

But less than fifteen minutes later, as the Reverend Uist Fergusson was inviting his congregation to rise to their feet and join together in praising the Lord with a hearty rendition of 'O Come All Ye Faithful', Isla's tranquillity was suddenly shattered. For it was then, as she stood up and opened her hymnal, that her eyes fell on the tall figure right at the front. Every muscle in her body went rigid. Somehow she had not expected Rory to be here.

He was dressed in the same black overcoat as before, the thin line of a burgundy Paisley silk scarf separating the blackness of his hair from the blackness of his collar. As he turned slightly to pass a hymn book to the woman at his side, Isla caught a glimpse of his arrogant dark profile before she hastily snatched her eyes away. Why couldn't he have stayed at home? she thought unchristianly.

Why did he have to spoil this special evening for her?

The presence of the woman was almost equally unsettling, for it was Elizabeth Buchanan, Rory's mother, the woman who all those years ago had been so violently opposed to her son's liaison with a lowly MacDonald and who had made absolutely no secret of the fact. In her heart Isla had always partly blamed her for the disintegration of her relationship with Rory. Elizabeth Buchanan was a tough, determined woman, known for her ability to get her own way.

But there was no sign of Evelyn, Isla realised as, a moment later, she made a quick, discreet check. Perhaps Elizabeth had finally taken her son over totally, even to the exclusion of his wife!

Had it not been for the presence of the Buchanans, Isla would have thoroughly enjoyed the service. The Reverend Fergusson had an inspiring touch. His sermon, as always, kept the whole church spellbound. As it was, however, Isla was only too grateful when, with a final blessing, the service was ended and the congregation began to file outside again.

Isla slipped an arm through one each of her parents' and tried to sound casual as they stepped out into the snow. 'Let's get out of here quickly, before the place gets jammed up with traffic. I'm dying for a hot drink and bed.'

But, though her parents might have been willing to oblige, custom and the mood of the season were destined to scupper her plans for a hasty retreat. They had barely got halfway to the car park when her parents were besieged by a group of assorted neighbours, wishing them a Merry Christmas and enquiring after her father's health. There was nothing for it but to pause for a chat.

And that, of course, was when it happened, just as Isla had feared it would. As she stood on the periphery of the little group, keeping her eyes fixed straight ahead, suddenly there was a light touch on her shoulder and a deep voice enquired, 'Did you enjoy the service?'

Isla spun round, her face dark with annoyance as she looked into a pair of deep tawny eyes. 'The service was excellent.' Her tone was hostile. 'But I really have no desire to discuss it with you.'

Rory smiled a wry smile, his dark brows lifting in criticism. 'Still the same old irascible Isla, I see. Whatever happened to Christmas cheer?'

'Christmas cheer?' She met his eyes levelly. 'You're the last person with any right to talk to me of Christmas cheer! What has Christmas cheer to do with what you're doing to my parents?'

In the crisp midnight darkness with the snow coming down to rest like a caress on his dark hair and shoulders, he had a look of the old, untamed Rory about him, and, in spite of herself, she felt a lance drive through her.

She would never again, as long as the lived, know a man as exciting as Rory had been. And, though it pained her to admit it, she knew deep within her that neither would she ever love again as she had loved him. Only once in a lifetime could any human heart experience a love so reckless and so overpowering. For though a heart might love again, it would love more wisely, with more caution, always careful to keep a safe distance. No heart dared risk, twice in a lifetime, its own near-total annihilation.

With these thoughts suddenly raging like a tempest within her, Isla continued to scowl at him, the author of her tragedy. Had she never loved him and he never betrayed her, she might not be in the lonely state in which she found herself today. She would long ago have found another man, a man she could have loved and who would have loved her, a man who might have made her happy.

Instead, as her mother had so wisely pointed out, she seemed doomed forever to search in all the wrong places. To go stumbling down endless blind romantic alleys, half knowing that what drew her to all those unavailable men was the very fact of their unavailability, yet unable to do a thing about it. For were she to be confronted by a man who could be hers for the asking, she knew she would run a million miles.

A heart might love again, but it must first learn to trust. And, trusting, take the risk of that ultimate giving. And that was the barrier Isla had never overcome in all the years since Rory had betrayed her.

How could she trust again when history might repeat itself? How could she dare love again, even a little?

Through the tumult in her heart she barely heard what he was saying, as he told her, 'That's what I want to speak to you about.'

Isla frowned at him, hating him. 'I don't know what you're talking about!'

Rory regarded her levelly through his golden eagle eyes, his expression a composed antithesis of her own. 'I'm talking about that small matter you came to see me about in my office the other afternoon.' He glanced expressively around him. 'But we can't discuss it here. We can discuss it over lunch the day after Boxing Day. I'll pick you up at the cottage at one o'clock.'

Then, before Isla could say a word, he had turned away and was leaning towards the little group of friends and neighbours to address her parents with total aplomb. 'Merry Christmas, Mrs MacDonald. Merry Christmas, Mr MacDonald. I'm glad to see you out and about again.'

As his greetings were returned, he began to move away, but not without a final glance at Isla.

'One o'clock sharp. Don't keep me waiting—at least, not if you want to resolve the problem.' Then, oblivious to the pair of violet eyes that were piercing into his back like daggers, he turned calmly on his heel and strode off into the snow.

Buchanan of Strathallane had spoken. And his will, as ever, would be done.

'It looks as though you've won him round, after all!' Isobel MacDonald could scarcely contain her excitement when, back home that evening, Isla told her about her coming lunch date with Rory. She hugged her daughter warmly. 'I knew you'd do it! I knew you'd manage to talk him round.'

'I haven't done it yet,' Isla was quick to warn her. 'Better not count your chickens. All he said was that he wanted to discuss it. He didn't say anything about having changed his plans.'

But Isobel MacDonald had total faith in her daughter. 'He will once you've had another chat with him. He wouldn't have asked to see you if he wasn't already having second thoughts.'

That was what it looked like, even to Isla, instinctively sceptical though she was regarding Rory's motives. 'We'll see,' she grumbled, half to herself, her spirits leaden at the prospect of having to confront him again. 'I just wish, though, that he hadn't insisted on lunch.' A quick half-hour in his office might have been a little less unpalatable. 'I think he had a nerve to do that.'

'The office is probably closed over Christmas and New Year,' Isobel sensibly pointed out to her. 'I think it's very civil of him to suggest that you discuss it over lunch.'

'Civil?' Isla could not quite suppress a mocking laugh. 'When did Rory Buchanan ever behave civilly towards me?'

The rough reminder of the past was not lost on her mother. She reached across and gently touched her daughter's hand. 'You mustn't think of such things, my dear. That's all behind you long ago. This is nothing but a simple little business lunch.' Then she frowned a little and added earnestly, 'But if it's going to upset you, you mustn't go. The last thing I want is for you to be hurt.'

'Of course I'll go.' Isla smiled at her mother, shaking off the bitterness within her. 'Don't worry, it's a long time since Rory had the power to hurt me. And, as you say, it's nothing but a simple little business lunch.'

All the same, the prospect of that simple little business lunch lurked in Isla's consciousness like an unwelcome visitor throughout the Christmas celebrations, although she was at pains not to let her parents see it. For she knew that, had they seriously suspected her anguish, they would instantly have banned her from going through with it, even if it had meant that building would go ahead tomorrow.

And that was something she could not allow to happen. For, after all, what was a lunch date? At worst, a couple of hours of perfect torture and then, God willing, she need never set eyes on him again. It was a small enough sacrifice to make. And perhaps, when at the end of it she had finally won him over, he would be flushed forever out of her system.

The need for such an outcome seemed greater than ever when, on Christmas night, she suffered the nightmare.

It was the same nightmare that had haunted her for years and which tended to descend when she was feeling anxious or when she had had recent contact with Rebecca, her sister's daughter, and this time both factors came into play. For on Christmas afternoon Heather had phoned from Antwerp to wish them all a merry Christmas and in the course of the phone call Isla had said a few words to Rebecca. She had not really been surprised when the nightmare had come.

In every detail it had been the same as usual. She was lost in a forest, carrying a bundle, knowing that there was something precious inside. She paused beneath the trees to open the bundle and there in her arms was a tiny baby. As the baby smiled at her she saw at once that it was Rebecca and, instantly, a great sorrow flooded through her.

For it was not her sister's daughter she longed to gaze on, but her own child, hers and Rory's.

As had happened each time, she had awakened, weeping, and she had had to lie quietly for a very long time before she could stop her limbs from trembling.

Each time the dream came to her she prayed it would be the last, and this time even more than ever. Surely this demon had run its course? Surely the time had come for her to break free from it?

All these hopes and fears and secret anxieties were lying dormant and tightly controlled within her as, already dressed in her navy boots and coat, she stood by the parlour window on the day after Boxing Day, the time one minute to one o'clock, waiting for Rory's car to appear.

Outwardly, she was her usual composed, unruffled self. Inwardly, she felt frayed and tattered. She had rashly thought she would enjoy this battle with him, but already she was rapidly losing the taste for it.

'There he is now!' Suddenly her mother was at her elbow as the silver-grey Jaguar drew up silently outside the gate.

Isla grabbed her bag and headed for the front door, snatching her parents each a fleeting kiss as she went. 'Keep your fingers crossed!' she implored them, pulling the door open. 'I promise you I'll do my best.'

Her mother came scuttling to the door behind her. 'We'll be thinking of you, love,' she promised. Then she paused in the doorway to watch with a proud smile her daughter's unhurried, almost regal passage down the snow-covered path to the waiting car, little realising the storm of tangled emotions that raged and tore within that brave and battered heart.

As Isla stepped through the wrought-iron gate, with perfect timing, Rory climbed out of the car and came round to open the passenger door for her. An unnecessary gesture, Isla thought with irritation as, ignoring his greeting and avoiding his eyes, she slid into the warm, leather-scented interior. Perhaps the gesture had been for his amusement. Another bitter little touch for 'old times' sake'. For in the old days it had been a quirky and endearing quality of his that he always opened doors for her.

Now, however, she found nothing endearing about him. His moves were too calculated these days to be endearing. As she caught his quick nod in the direction of her mother, whose reaction was to scuttle hurriedly back indoors again, this impression seemed more than amply vindicated. He had always had charm, and once she had thought it was spontaneous. She had learned to her cost that it was merely a weapon.

As he slid into the seat beside her, a tall, sinuous figure in a dark blue suit, she caught a sudden sharp tang of the warm, clean scent of him, and for some reason that added to her growing irritation. She turned sharply to look at him, violet eyes like daggers. 'I want you to know that I find this lunch idea preposterous. Whatever it is you have to say, you could have told me over the phone or in your office. The only reason I'm here is because you gave me no option.'

The engine of the big car was running, but he hesitated as he reached to push the gear lever into first. He turned to look unblinkingly at her. 'If you had such strong objections,' he observed, 'you should have got in touch and cancelled.'

'Got in touch?' The suggestion irked her. 'How was I supposed to get in touch? Perhaps it has escaped your notice that this is Christmas. Your office, like everyone else's, is closed for the holidays.'

He smiled at her sarcasm. 'No, it had not escaped my notice. But I would have expected a high-ranking journalist like yourself to be a little more resourceful. My office is not the only place one can reach me. I also happen to have a phone at home.'

As the tawny eyes drove into her, Isla felt her own gaze waver, taken aback as much as anything by the impropriety of his suggestion. 'I'm sorry,' she pointed out, 'but I'm not in the habit of making phone calls to the homes of people with whom my dealings are of a purely business nature. Especially,' she elaborated, looking him straight in the eye, 'when the person in question happens to be a married man.'

His hand was still hovering over the gear lever as for a long time he looked back at her without saying a word. Then at last he spoke. 'Point taken,' he observed flatly, his tone as inscrutable as the expression in his eyes. Then he raised one black eyebrow and faced her squarely. 'It's still not too late to change your mind.' He waved one hand indifferently in the direction of the passenger door. 'If you'd rather just forget it, all you have to do is leave.'

And where would that leave her? Back where she started, with her parents' problem unresolved. She stared glacially back at him. 'I think it's rather late for that. Now that we're here we may as well get on with it.' Apart from the fact that her parents were relying on her, it went singularly against the grain to walk away now, empty-handed, after all the unpleasantness she'd already put herself through. 'I just wanted you to know,' she added crisply, 'that I would rather you hadn't insisted on lunch.'

'Objection noted.' To her annoyance, he smiled. 'So, now that you've got all that off your chest, do you think we can be on our way—or are there any more points you'd like to make first?'

Pointedly, Isla swivelled round in her seat, stiff-backed, to stare out through the windscreen. 'I'm waiting for you,' she told him caustically. 'You're the one who's making a fuss.'

She heard him laugh softly at her side as he pushed the gear lever into first, and at the sheer insensitive arrogance of him her lips pursed tightly in annoyance. Already, she was bristling like an angry porcupine and her ordeal hadn't even started yet! Perhaps, she thought as the big car moved off, she ought to have backed out when she'd still had the chance.

Don't be silly, it's only a business lunch, she told herself firmly as she scowled out at the road, and you've coped with hundreds of business lunches in your time.

But no amount of rationalisation could immunise her against the disruptive presence of the composed dark figure at her side. And no matter how hard she fought to quell it her heart went on ticking like a time bomb in her chest.

CHAPTER FOUR

Isla had expected Rory to take the road into town, but instead he was heading west across the Vale of Strathallane.

With a flicker of impatience she turned to look at him. 'Where are you taking me?' she demanded. Couldn't he, just once in his life, behave predictably?

Rory glanced across at her with devilment in his eyes. 'You'll see soon enough. It's just another few miles.'

'Why can't we just go to a restaurant in town? Surely that would be a great deal quicker?'

'Unarguably it would.' He turned back to his driving. 'But since neither of us is in a hurry, I thought it would be nice to drive somewhere a little further afield.' He flicked a mocking glance at her implacable profile as she turned once more to glare out through the windscreen. 'At least, I was assuming you had no further appointments today. You'd better tell me if you're in a hurry to get back.'

'No particular hurry.' Her tone was clipped. 'Though I see no need for this to take any longer than is absolutely necessary.'

Again she was aware of that soft, mocking laugh as he leaned forward to switch on the CD player. 'Not one minute longer than necessary,' he assured her, relaxing back a little in his seat as the opening bars of a Verdi overture wafted from the speakers. 'That I can absolutely guarantee.'

Isla folded her arms across her chest. 'Good,' she said, still staring straight ahead of her. 'I can assure you that's a great weight off my mind.'

In fact, she was not really reassured at all, though she was uncertain just why she was feeling so on edge. Possibly it was the false intimacy of their situation, she decided, discreetly inching her knees to one side. For she was aware that there was something faintly disturbing about being locked alone in the car with him. As they sped across the deserted, snow-covered landscape, sharing the warmth and the comfort of their private little capsule, it felt almost as though they were alone in the world. And that was a pretty intimate feeling.

A foolish one, too, Isla sharply reminded herself, and one she had no business entertaining. She had shared a car with a man a thousand times before and never been assailed by such fanciful ravings.

Yet it was impossible to deny she was painfully aware of the physical nearness of the man beside her. Even without her looking at him her consciousness was filled with the overpowering masculine aura of him. The powerful thighs beneath the fabric of his trousers that moved supplely with every brake and gear change, the long, tanned fingers that manipulated the gear lever, and the broad shoulders and strong arms whose muscles flexed a little with every twist and turn of the steering-wheel.

She could even in her mind's eye envisage the dark profile as he concentrated on the road ahead. The head of dark hair brushed back from his forehead, the straight black brows, the slightly crooked nose, broken long ago in a rugby tackle. And the golden eagle eyes with their fringe of dark lashes, that were like no other eyes she had ever looked into.

As she gazed at the picture in her mind, it suddenly occurred to her that she had been caught in a time warp. Sitting here beside him in this car had taken her back on the wings of memory to those earlier days they had spent together. That was why, without even looking at him, she was able to see and sense him so vividly.

In those days she had not been afraid to look at him. On the contrary, shamelessly, she would feast her eyes upon him, drinking in the power, the beauty, the excitement of him, her senses intoxicated by what she saw. And the memory of that time and of what he had been to her was scorched indelibly over her brain.

More fool you then and more fool you now, she admonished herself harshly, cutting the fantasy short. At least then you had the genuine excuse of innocence. You trusted him. You didn't know he was just leading you on. Now it was like an insult to all the suffering he had caused her that she should even for one moment have the bad taste to relive in her memory the passionate love she had once felt for him.

But at least, now that she had faced it, the moment had passed. As he turned off the main road through a pair of stone gateposts, that aura of intimacy, which had been but a figment of her imagination, had miraculously and thankfully vanished. For the moment at least he was just another man.

'We're here.'

As he spoke, they were coming to the end of a long gravelled driveway, approaching the forecourt of a stately greystone building. As Isla recognised it instantly, anger stirred within her. Now *he* was the one guilty of a lapse of taste! For this was none other than Kirkhaven Castle, a place she had last set foot in just over eight years ago.

As Rory parked the Jaguar by the castle wall, she wondered if he had chosen this venue deliberately, in an effort to undermine her composure. Or perhaps it had simply slipped his mind that it was at Kirkhaven Castle all those years ago that they had spent one of the most blissful nights of their romance, the first night, in fact, that they had ever spent together, the first night of that unforgettable pony-trekking holiday.

But there was no way of knowing what was passing through his mind as he reached behind him to grab his coat from the rear seat, then turned to her briefly before opening the driver's door. 'They do a very passable lunch here,' he observed without emotion. 'I come here fairly often with clients.'

'How nice for you.' Isla smiled coolly in response, lacing her tone with just a hint of irony. But, in truth, his pronouncement had been reassuring. It was essential that this fleeting renewal of their acquaintanceship be kept on a strictly business level. That way it would be easier for her to handle. It could be dangerous if they were to allow memories to intrude. Memories could lead to all sorts of complications.

But as she followed his lead and climbed out of the car, and watched him fling the dark coat over his shoulders before heading on long strides for the castle's main entrance, it was obvious that not the flicker of an uncomfortable memory troubled that practical and single-minded brain of his. Head high, Isla hurried across the gravel behind him. She would be wise to ensure that she was equally cold-blooded.

Kirkhaven Castle, a rambling sixteenth-century edifice, with fine views out over Lunan Bay, had been converted into a hotel in the 1930s. And it had been converted with a great deal of sensitivity and taste, all its old-world charm meticulously preserved, its former splendours magnificently restored. Stepping into the huge carpeted lobby, with its display of pikes and claymores on one wall, its heavy brocade hangings and aroma of polished wood, one could almost believe one had stepped back in time to when the place had been inhabited by local clan chieftains.

Isla felt her heart lift with pride and pleasure as she glanced round at the paintings and the coats of arms on the walls. To be in the midst of all this local history gave her an unexpected sense of belonging that ran far more deeply than any fragile memories that, had things been different, she might have shared with Rory.

Feeling oddly strengthened by this insight, she followed his broad back across the lobby, then through an archway into the dining-room.

'Your coat, madam.' A waiter was instantly upon them. 'Nice to see you again, sir. Did you have a good Christmas?'

As Rory nodded in response, Isla smiled to herself. Judging by the depth of the bow that had accompanied the waiter's solicitous enquiry, Buchanan of Strathallane was a revered and valued customer. Things had indeed changed since eight years ago when he had been treated just the same as anyone else.

Their coats taken care of, they were led to a table by one of the soaring casement windows with a view out over the silvery bay.

'Will you have a drink to start, sir?' The waiter went on hovering as he handed them each a large tasselled menu.

'I'll have my usual.' Rory glanced across at Isla. 'And for the young lady, a——'

'Dry martini,' Isla supplied.

As the waiter took his leave, Rory glanced out of the window. 'It's a pity you have to see it at this time of the year.' He indicated with a gesture the snowy landscape that fringed the silver-grey of the bay. 'It's really very beautiful in summer.'

So, he *had* forgotten. A shaft of pain went through her, totally unexpected, making her tense perceptibly. But it seemed he had failed to notice her reaction as he went on in a faintly damning tone, 'Still, I expect it's a bit of a novelty for you. Rather different, I imagine, from the restaurants you're used to in London.'

It was a million light years away from the sort of watering holes she was used to. In London one frequented restaurants almost exclusively for the food. Surroundings and décor were of minor importance. But a meal at Kirkhaven Castle would be a memorable experience—and not just for the food, for the whole package that went with it.

But she was not about to be lavish in her praise to Rory. In fact, if she could succeed in offending him a little, as he a moment ago had offended her, she would derive a measure of satisfaction. In a clipped tone she informed him, 'If you're trying to impress me, you might have saved yourself the bother. I'm here to discuss business. The view doesn't matter a damn to me. For all I care about all this splendid "novelty", as you call it, you could have saved yourself some money and taken me to a hamburger bar!'

Rory regarded her for a long silent moment as a botanist might regard some unfamiliar species. Then he sat back in his seat and narrowed his tawny eyes at her. 'I'll remember that in future,' he observed laconically. 'For the moment, alas, you'll have to make do with this. There are no hamburger bars that I know of in Strathallane.'

Isla glanced down quickly at her menu. She had not offended him, she had simply amused him with her vitriolic little outburst.

'Besides,' he added, rubbing salt in, 'I would say you're rather overdressed for a quick stop off at a hamburger bar.'

As he spoke, his eyes travelled quite openly over her, assessing the dark blue silk crêpe de Chine blouse she wore and the slim-cut matching dark blue skirt. At her throat a gold chain necklace glistened, its lustre echoed by the matching earrings in her ears.

'Not that I'm complaining,' he added wickedly, as his eyes moved lazily once more to her face. 'It makes a very pleasant change to have a bit of elegant female company.'

Isla looked back at him, her gaze steady and damning. 'I'm sure your wife would love to hear you saying that.' She caught the momentary reaction deep in his eyes—a flash of irritation followed by a hint of withdrawal—and took pleasure in pursuing her momentary advantage. 'I'm afraid I'm not here to provide you with a pleasant change, however. As I said before, I'm here simply to discuss business.'

The waiter chose that moment to arrive with their drinks, a whisky with a jug of Highland water for Rory, a perfectly mixed martini for Isla.

Rory poured a small measure of the water into his drink, took a long, slow mouthful then laid the glass down again. 'I suggest you take a look at the menu,' he told her. 'Then we can order and get down to business.'

There was a harsh note in his voice that was mostly anger, yet laced with some other emotion Isla could not quite identify and which caused her to glance curiously across at him for a moment. But he did not meet her eyes. He had bent to study his menu, his features a closed and impenetrable mask. He had not taken kindly to that reference to his wife. More than likely it had aroused an unwelcome sense of guilt in view of that deliberate attempt at flirtation.

That was all to the good, Isla decided, as she too turned her attention to the menu. Let there be not the slightest confusion as to where they stood on that particular issue.

They ordered salmon to start with and steaks to follow, a light Sancerre to drink with the fish and a full-bodied burgundy to complement the steaks. Then, as the waiter left them, Rory drained his whisky, sat back in his seat and looked across at Isla. 'I suppose you're wondering what it is I wanted to talk to you about? Allow me to enlighten you.'

As he paused for a second, Isla cut in. 'I presume it's about the matter of Jock Campbell's field and my request to you to halt your plans to build on it?'

Rory raised one dark eyebrow. 'Not exactly,' he told her.

Instantly, Isla felt herself stiffen. Had he brought her here under false pretences? She might have known he would be incapable of dealing straight with her. She looked him in the eye and demanded impatiently, 'And what exactly is "not exactly" supposed to mean?'

'It means that what I brought you here to discuss is something rather different. Namely, a favour I'd like to ask of you.'

Isla regarded him suspiciously. 'What sort of a favour? I can think of none that I would be prepared to do voluntarily for you.'

Rory simply smiled. 'This one you might. In fact I would be most surprised if you refused.'

As he spoke, he toyed idly with his fork, his long fingers dark against the spotless gleaming silver, and in spite of herself Isla found herself following the supple, seductive movements of his hand, reflecting how perfect was the line of his light blue shirt against the strong, hair-roughened wrist. Then, in horror at herself, she snatched her eyes away, just as he was saying, 'Don't you want to know what it is?'

'I think I understand.' All at once it had come to her. 'You want me to do some favour for you before you'll agree to my demands?' She gave a cynical laugh as she looked across at him. 'I might have known you would demand your pound of flesh.'

Rory shrugged. 'I'm a businessman, remember? I don't believe in trading something for nothing. It's my policy always to balance the books.'

'I'll bet it is.' She met his gaze with condemnation. 'No doubt with a little on the credit side in your own favour.'

He did not disagree, he simply smiled that amused, superior smile of his. 'So, would you like me to explain exactly what I have in mind for you? I promise you it's something you'll rather enjoy.'

'Your salmon, madam.' The waiter had reappeared soundlessly and was laying a plate of smoked salmon before her.

Isla kept her eyes fixed implacably on Rory. What exactly was he getting at? She felt a sudden tug of apprehension. It would not be the first time in her life that some man had offered to do her a favour in exchange for favours of a more intimate nature. If that was the sort of trade-off Rory had in mind he was destined, like them, for a disappointment— not to mention also a verbal mauling he was never likely to forget.

Only in Rory's case she was prepared to go even further. Vindictively she eyed the salmon the waiter had set before him. If he had the infinite gall even to suggest such a thing, he would end up with a plate of Loch Fyne salmon over his head!

As the waiter departed, she leaned towards him across the table, eyes narrowed, fingers twitching in anticipation. 'Well? I'm waiting,' she demanded.

He picked up the silver fork and knife and carefully broke off a piece of pink flesh. 'What I hope to do is draw upon your special talents.' He held her eyes as he transferred the salmon unhurriedly to his mouth. 'I know from personal experience what a natural you are in this area, and your talent, quite clearly, has matured with the years.'

Was it her imagination or, as he spoke, did his eyes drift downwards to her breasts and pause for a moment to graze their firm contours that pressed against the soft silk of her blouse? Was she mistaken or had his voice all at once dropped an octave, his tone husky and inviting to her ear? And as he laid down his cutlery and reached for his napkin did the long, tanned fingers seem to move with the sensuous languor of a caress?

She clenched her fists and demanded almost shrilly, 'Kindly stop going round in circles! Get to the point! What are you talking about?'

His eyes widened a fraction in surprise at her reaction. He touched the napkin to his mouth. 'I thought it was obvious. Your special talent, Isla dear, as we all know, is your ability as a journalist.'

After that incredible build-up it was almost an anticlimax. As she stared back at him, suddenly feeling quite limp inside, Isla was aware that her mouth had gone dry. She reached for her wine glass and swallowed back a mouthful and instantly felt a little better. 'And what possible interest could you have,' she demanded, 'in my ability as a journalist?'

'Don't tell me you've forgotten——' his tone was almost teasing '—that it was at Buchanan's that you began your illustrious career?'

As his eyes met hers and held them for a moment, instantly, against her will, Isla was transported back to the *Juliet* office where she had gone to work when she had first left school. She could see the wooden desks with their old-fashioned typewriters, the fondly remembered faces of her colleagues—and, most vividly of all, the tall figure of Rory in the doorway, all eager smiles, warm lips and caresses, waiting to whisk her off somewhere.

For a moment the strength of the memory stunned her. It seemed to tear at her insides and rip them apart. She felt a mute sob of pain rise up in her throat and she had to swallow hard before it could choke her.

This is ridiculous, pathetic, she chided herself miserably. You haven't thought of any of these things for years! They're dead, they're over! Don't think of them now!

With an effort she clambered back into the present. 'Of course I remember,' she agreed with composure. 'But I still don't understand what it is you're getting at.'

'That's because I haven't told you yet.' He smiled at her disarmingly, making her heart squeeze. 'I'm just about to do so now.'

Isla picked up her fork and knife—anything to avoid eye contact—and pretended to divert her attention to her food. 'Go ahead. I'm listening,' she said.

Rory paused to take a mouthful of his wine. 'Let me start by explaining the problem,' he put to her. 'It's a problem that I've seen coming over the years, but have been too busy to deal with directly.' He laid down his glass. 'As, of course, you already know, Buchanan's began as a publishing house and that was really all we were until fairly recently. With our limited number of publications, however, we could never have hoped to survive into the nineties, let alone into the twenty-first century. Fortunately, thanks to a policy of diversification, our survival is no longer in question.'

As he paused, Isla allowed herself a wry smile. What an uncharacteristic display of modesty! This 'we' he was talking about was entirely mythical. The spectacular blossoming of Buchanan's fortunes had been down to one man and one man only. And, as the whole world knew, that man was Rory. She raised her eyes to his as he continued,

'Unfortunately, in the process, the publishing side has been neglected. We still have the same half-dozen titles as before and their circulation, frankly, is declining. What we need is an injection of new blood, new ideas, fresh inspiration. Without detracting at all from the talents of the staff who have been running our magazines for the past few years, I have to say that most of them are a little out of touch with what's happening in the world today. Hardly surprising.' He paused and smiled. 'A large proportion of them are within a decade of retirement.'

Isla chewed thoughtfully on her salmon, her suspicions growing as to where his arguments were leading. Yet her composed expression revealed nothing as she raised one eyebrow and enquired of him, 'So?'

'So...' His salmon finished, he laid down his knife and fork and touched his napkin lightly to his lips. 'About eighteen months ago I got together a team of our younger editorial staff and put them to work to devise a new magazine. They got as far as producing a dummy when, just before the summer, the editor left.' He pulled a wry smile as he dropped his napkin on to the table-top. 'The lure of London. I didn't blame her. But, unfortunately, it left the project in the lurch.'

'Couldn't you have promoted one of the others? One of the others who were working on the new magazine?'

Rory shrugged a small shrug. 'I suppose I could have done, but frankly I didn't think any of them were up to it. That sort of position requires very special skills—creativity and management know-how, not to mention an instinct for the market, all wrapped up in one energetic person. But I don't need to tell you that. That's your business.'

There was an edge of flattery to his tone as he glanced across the table-top, his tawny eyes smiling, but Isla was not about to be seduced by soft words. She looked him straight in the eye and told him frankly, 'If you're thinking of offering me a job, you can forget it. I wouldn't work for you if you were the last publishing company on earth.'

Rory leaned back a little in his chair and folded his arms lightly across his chest. 'As a matter of fact, I wasn't about to offer you a job,' he told her.

Isla smiled without humour. 'That's a relief.'

'As we both know and as I've already told you, London, amid the bright lights and the faceless millions, is where you naturally belong. Don't worry, I'm only too well aware that nothing could tear you away from all that.'

There was an unexpected ring of hostility in his voice, reminiscent of that previous time when he had attacked her. And, as then, it took Isla by surprise. What had *he* to be hostile about? *She* was the one with grudges to spare!

Her tone sharply defensive, she demanded, 'Then why all the build-up if you're not offering me a job? You can't surely believe I give a damn about your problems?'

Rory leaned towards her, his tawny eyes darkening. 'No, indeed. That's something I have never doubted. The only problems that have ever concerned you are your own.' Then he leaned back in his chair again as she glared at him, hating him, and continued in the same damning tone, 'However, since caring is not what we're here to talk about, such minor deficiencies need hardly concern us.'

He unfolded his arms irritably and narrowed his eyes at her. 'As I said at the beginning, I want you to do me a favour—in exchange for a possible favour from me. And what I would like you to do is very simple—namely, take a look at that dummy for the new magazine and tell me what you think of it.' His tawny eyes glinted as he continued to look across at her. 'That shouldn't be much of a problem for a hot-shot editor like you.'

On the surface, no. But Isla knew Rory well. How things appeared on the surface could be misleading. What mattered was what was underneath.

She threw him a canny look and enquired with some scepticism, 'All you want is my opinion? You wouldn't by any chance be expecting me to throw in a few ideas of my own?'

He responded with a smile that lightened his dark features and brought a twinkle to his eyes. 'All I'm really asking is that you give me your opinion as to whether you think this new magazine is worth going ahead with or not. However, if you felt like contributing a little something extra, I can't say I'd object in the least. Please don't feel restricted by your brief.'

In spite of herself, Isla smiled back at him. 'That's extremely generous of you,' she joked. 'However, I'm not sure that my employers would approve of such an arrangement. My contract forbids me to do work for anyone else without first seeking their consent.'

Rory shrugged. 'That's not a problem. This is purely an informal arrangement. You're simply doing a favour for an old friend.'

Hearing those words again brought her back down to earth. As the smile faded from her face, she felt moved to remind him that he was not and never had been any kind of friend of hers. But, annoyed at herself for her misplaced sensitivity, she pointed out to him instead, 'If I agree, it will of course be on condition that you do a corresponding favour for me. You must drop your plans to build on Jock Campbell's land.'

He regarded her obliquely. 'That won't be easy.'

'Easy or not, I'm afraid you must do it. It's the only way I'll agree to help you.'

Rory shrugged. 'I'll do what I can. But I'm afraid I'm not making any promises.'

'Then that's not good enough! You must promise! A deal's a deal. An agreement's an agreement!'

He did not answer her straight away, but the tawny eyes had grown as hard as boulders in the suddenly granite-carved lines of his face. 'I see you're issuing orders again. I've already told you that won't work with me.' His tone was rough gravel grinding in a cement mixer. 'Either you accept my offer that I shall try to accommodate you or we can just forget the whole thing right now.'

He really meant it. She could see it in his eyes. Sooner than be seen to bow to her demands, he would simply forgo the valuable service she could offer him. She cursed him to damnation beneath her breath, knowing he had caught her in an impossible trap. However vague his terms, she could not refuse him if there was even a small chance that he might eventually deliver. It was not some game, after all. Her parents' happiness was at stake.

'So you see,' he was saying, 'it's up to you. You're the one who has to decide.'

Isla was glad that at that moment the waiter arrived to clear away their plates. It allowed her a moment or two, she thought wryly, to capitulate with a measure of grace. She waited until he had served their steaks and filled up their glasses with glowing red burgundy, then with a deliberately cool look she caught Rory's eye.

'It beats me how you can dare to have confidence in your business associates if you make a habit of offering them such abysmally bad terms.'

Her mouth quirked with sarcasm as she added, 'I have, of course, no choice but to accept, but if you fail to return my favour with a favour, what's to stop me giving you bad advice?'

Rory smiled in response. 'You wouldn't do that. You care too much for your professional honour.' He smiled again, but his smile had a cold edge to it. 'Nothing is dearer to you than your professional reputation. I shall rest easy in my bed. You won't give me bad advice.'

He held out his hand to her across the table. 'So, it's a deal, then. We're finally partners. I look forward to a productive association.'

As they shook hands briefly, Isla snatched hers away, feeling almost as though he had stung her. And behind her stiff smile her heart was pounding as though it might burst through the walls of her chest. For suddenly it felt as though eight years of nightmares were crashing down about her head. He was the very worst thing that had ever happened to her, but somehow she had forgotten him and cast his treachery from her heart. And all she had ever asked of fate was that she might never set eyes on him again.

It had not been much to ask, she thought, weeping inwardly. Surely she'd deserved that much after the pain of her struggle.

And yet now this man who had brought her nothing but heartache and from whom she had fought so long and so painfully to be free, in the space of one fleeting and treacherous heartbeat, held her once more in the palm of his hand.

CHAPTER FIVE

'HERE'S your coffee, Miss MacDonald. And I brought you some biscuits just in case you'd like them.'

Isla glanced up from the sheaf of papers she was reading and smiled at the young secretary as she laid the tray on her desk. 'That's very kind of you, Jackie,' she offered. 'I was just starting to feel a little peckish.'

The girl flushed with pleasure as she headed for the door and Isla watched her go, slightly regretting the haughty way she had treated her on their very first meeting. In spite of her gauche, unpolished exterior, Rory's secretary was a treasure.

Isla reached for her coffee and took a mouthful. It was strong and black, just as she liked it. Then she leaned back in her chair and gazed at the window, reflecting that, all things considered, she'd had few causes for complaint over the past couple of days. There'd been endless cups of coffee and supplies of biscuits, not to mention her own office on the directorial third floor. All very different, she smiled to herself, from those earlier days at Buchanan's as a lowly sub-editor.

It had felt very strange coming back to work here, particularly since it was the last thing she had ever expected to do. But when Rory had offered her her own private little office, albeit just two doors along from his own, she had accepted his offer as the most sensible solution.

'I'll only be coming in for a couple of hours,' she had warned him. 'Just for as long as it takes me to read through that dummy.' But she knew she would work more efficiently in an office than she ever would have been able to at the cottage. Two hours in the office would be at least four at home.

Rory had smiled, a wise, knowing smile. 'Absolutely,' he had agreed, but with that twinkle in his eye that said he knew better. 'I wouldn't expect you to stay one minute longer than you need to.'

And his unspoken prophecy had been proved absolutely right. On her first day, yesterday, she had come in after lunch, fully expecting to be home before tea. It had been well after six when Rory had tapped on the door. 'Shall I give you a lift home or are you spending the night?'

The trouble was she was an addict for her work. Put Isla in an editorial office with a pile of copy and a blue pencil and she literaly didn't know when to stop. And, in spite of her firmly made resolution to treat this current assignment with contempt, two pages into the dummy she had been totally hooked.

She had spent the next four hours writing out copious notes and poring over every record sheet and file she could lay hands on. And that evening when Rory had dropped her off at the cottage she hadn't been able to wait for the next morning to get back behind her desk.

This morning her taxi had deposited her outside the Buchanan building just a little after nine o'clock. Somehow, today she just *had* to finish earlier. She had promised her mother faithfully that she would be home for tea.

She sighed now as she took another mouthful of her coffee. Perhaps she had been rash to make such a promise. Already it was after three o'clock and here she was, still scribbling away. As her stomach gurgled, she reached for a biscuit. And she hadn't even broken off for lunch!

Jackie had left the office door slightly ajar, and it creaked now, ever so softly, as someone pushed it open. Then, as Isla swivelled round curiously in her chair, a deep voice enquired, 'May I interrupt you for a moment? I was just wondering how you were getting on.'

Curiosity turned instantly to irritation. Her grip on her pencil tightened ferociously. 'I'd get on better if you didn't interrupt me. As it happens, I'm right in the middle of something.'

Her rebuke fell on blissfully insensitive ears. Without pausing in his stride, Rory crossed to her desk and perched himself casually on the end of it. Then, smiling down at her with unrepentant eyes, he unbuttoned the jacket of his mid-grey suit. The tie at his throat was a rich, deep claret, the shirt he wore immaculate white. And the lights and darks of the sharply contrasting colours dramatically enhanced his striking dark looks.

Against the collar of his shirt his dark hair curled crisply. Gleaming ebony against sparkling snow-white. And somehow the warm notes in his tie lent an added depth and fire to the dark tawny eyes. As he momentarily adjusted the cuff of his shirt, his fingers flashed darkly against the starched cotton. For, whatever movement he made, the eye nat-

urally followed it. Visually, he was not an easy man
to ignore.

And yet, as she had always felt with Rory, Isla
was acutely aware that the elegant outer wrapping
was entirely superfluous. It was some unique inner
quality of the man, his proud, confident bearing
and raw animal energy that automatically commanded the attention. Eyes would swing naturally
in the direction of Rory whether he was dressed in
Savile Row made to measure or decked out in rags.

As she sought to reject this faintly galling truth,
she was aware that he was looking down at her.

'Jackie tells me you sent down for all the files—
editorial, market research, even the production
figures.' There was a glint of amusement in the
golden eagle eyes. 'I'm very flattered that you're
taking your task so seriously.'

'Then don't be.' Isla's tone was crisp. 'I can assure
you there's no cause for you to feel flattered just
because I take pride in doing a job properly.' As
she spoke, she leaned back a little in her chair and
twisted a stray strand of glossy chestnut hair carefully behind her ear. It was a nervous gesture, but,
damn it, he made her nervous! Somehow his very
presence undermined her.

Then immediately, to counterbalance any wrong
impression, she raised one perfectly pencilled
eyebrow and looked him ferociously in the eye.
'Was there anything in particular you wanted to ask
me about? Perhaps I could enlighten you and then
you could be on your way?'

'I'm in no hurry.' His tone was teasing. Her
'eyebrow' treatment, needless to say, had been no
more effective this time than it had before. He

folded his arms across his chest and continued to watch her with irritating amusement. 'So, this is what a big city editor looks like.' He allowed his eyes to drift slowly over her, making her cheeks glow as warmly as the cherry-red of her sweater dress. 'I've always wondered what a high-powered London editor looked like at work.'

'Well, now you know.' Isla bit the words at him. It appeared he had found himself with time on his hands and had decided it would be amusing to stop by and bait her. 'And if that was all you wanted to find out, I suggest that, now that your curiosity has been satisfied, there's really nothing more to keep you. You may be in no hurry, but I am.' She glanced very pointedly at her watch and tapped her pencil impatiently on the desk. 'I'd like to get finished and be home in time for tea.'

Rory shrugged broad shoulders and continued to look at her, apparently with not the faintest intention of leaving. 'You're free to go whenever you like. You could pack up this very minute if you want to.'

'I'm afraid I can't. I haven't finished. I told you already, I'm right in the middle of something.'

Predictably Rory ignored her subtle hint and reached for one of the files that were piled in front of her. Idly he thumbed through it and then enquired without looking at her, 'So, what conclusions have you come to? What's your impression of this new magazine?'

'I haven't come to any conclusions yet. As I keep telling you, I'm still working on it.'

Rory glanced across at her stiff, angry face and for a long, still moment seemed to study her. Then he laid down the file, his movements unhurried, and enquired in a low voice, 'What's happened to you, Isla? You used to have a sense of humour.'

He paused for a moment, the tawny eyes narrowing, and he seemed to sigh beneath his breath as he added, 'All this professional success of yours seems to have changed you—and that, I can assure you, would be a most dreadful pity. I hope you'll forgive me for saying so, but you seem in danger of taking yourself just a little too seriously.'

There was an unexpected warmth and familiarity in his tone that caught at her heart-strings and tugged them shamelessly. And the way he had looked at her, as though he really cared for her, had brought a hard lump to her throat. It reminded her of the way he once used to speak and look at her. The memory of such tenderness was almost unbearably painful.

But this time there had been pity in his voice as well. Pity and a sprinkling of condescension. And it was to these that Isla instantly responded. She glared at him with indignation. 'You are, of course, entitled to your opinion. I'm so sorry you disapprove of what you believe I have become.' In spite of herself, her voice was shaking. 'However, it appears not to have occurred to you that the feeling just might be mutual.'

Their eyes clashed like cymbals across the desktop, then with a small sigh Rory shook his head. 'Point taken,' he agreed with the lift of one dark eyebrow. 'Neither of us these days is much enamoured of the other. What else can one expect after all these years?'

The passage of years had nothing to do with her feelings for him. Indeed, in eight years they had hardly changed, except perhaps to harden a little. Hating him had become a way of life. But she was not about to enter into a debate. All that mattered was that he understood that his dislike was fully reciprocated.

He seemed less than devastated by the revelation. No more irked than a man discovering a small pebble in his shoe. As she continued to glare at him, he observed in a mocking tone, 'Now that we've dealt with all the social niceties, how about getting back to business? I'm anxious to know what you think of our magazine. On its success or failure could hang the future of my plans to expand the publishing side of things.'

He paused to fix her with a cruelly amused look. 'Plans, of course, which will require an enlargement of our premises. Possibly the construction of a new annexe.' He smiled at her devilishly. 'I have a site in mind—but that, of course, is another story.'

When Isla did not reply, but simply glared at him, he reiterated smoothly, 'So, what's your verdict? What's your impression of the new magazine?'

Isla took a deep breath, her violet eyes hostile, and regarded him resentfully for a moment. If that last remark had been meant to unnerve her and subtly remind her of where she stood, it had hit its target more or less dead centre. Just the thought of an annexe of Buchanan's coming into being in her parents' back yard had instantly made her lose her taste for evasion. All her attitude had succeeded in doing was annoy him. She would perhaps be wiser just to answer his question.

She glanced down at her desk to compose her reply. 'I think, basically, it's on the right track,' she told him. 'It has very definite possibilities. In my opinion, at the moment there's a gap in the market that such a magazine could make a good job of filling.'

His eyes were on her, absorbing every word. 'But you have reservations about it as it stands?' he coaxed.

Isla nodded. 'I do. Quite serious reservations. At the moment it lacks a clear-cut image of itself. Here and there it lacks the courage of its convictions. It risks ending up being neither one thing nor the other.'

Rory was still seated on the edge of the desk, his expression rapt as he continued to encourage her. 'So, where, specifically, would you say it's going wrong?'

Isla frowned thoughtfully before answering. 'There are several areas I'm not too happy with. The tenor of some of the features to start with . . .' She flicked through the heap of papers on her desk and quickly drew out the ones she was looking for. 'This sort of thing.' She handed them to him. 'I suppose it's valid enough, but it's dated. All this hammering on about women's lib issues doesn't appeal to the average reader any more.'

She paused and glanced up quickly to look at him, half expecting some chauvinistic comment. 'I'm not suggesting that women's rights are not an important issue, but they have to be presented rather differently today. More in the context of human rights in general.'

Rory continued to scan the pages she had given him and nodded in agreement. 'Yes, I see what you mean.' And from the sober, respectful expression on his face the comment she had half expected had not even passed through his head. He nodded again and raised narrowed tawny eyes to her. 'So, what else, apart from the features?' he enquired.

'Well, I think it needs brightening up visually,' Isla answered. 'The graphics need to be bolder, to give it a bit more zest, and the layouts need to be a bit more daring. Some are very good as they stand,' she amended quickly, pulling another sheet unerringly from the pile before her to illustrate her case. 'But others...' She searched for and found another piece of evidence and handed both of them to Rory. 'With others, the design seems to have lost its nerve.'

'You're right. This one really catches the eye, whereas this one looks boring before you even start reading.'

'It's because of the way it's been laid out.' Isla leaned towards him and pointed with her pencil. 'This title is lost here at the top of the page. It should be placed centre and the illustration should be blown up and placed down at the bottom, here.' In her enthusiasm she had half risen from her seat and was barely aware of how close to him she was standing. It was only as her arm brushed lightly against his sleeve, sending a warm electric pulse rushing through her, that she stiffened slightly and drew away. 'That would be one way of improving it,' she finished off lamely.

Rory, however, seemed quite unaware of her lapse. He appeared genuinely absorbed in their discussion. 'I'll tell you something else that worried me personally. The style of cover. It just didn't strike me as right.'

In spite of herself, Isla felt genuinely impressed. She had supposed that this project was of no real interest to him, just something he had decided ought to be done. A gesture towards tradition, more than anything, a nod of respect for what Buchanan's had once been.

It was a surprise to discover that his involvement was genuine and that he had actually taken the trouble to appraise himself of the details. It was even more of a surprise—or, more precisely, a shock—that for his major criticism he should home in so accurately on the point that had also been troubling her most.

When before, she thought almost bitterly, had their two minds ever thought alike?

She reseated herself carefully before taking up his point. For all at once then she had had the feeling that she was working *with* him, rather than just *for* him, and there was something distinctly uncomfortable about that.

Taking care to hide her feelings and keep her tone professional, she answered him. 'Yes, I tend to agree with you. In my opinion, the cover needs to be totally rethought. At the moment it's lacking in any kind of originality.'

Rory nodded. 'That was my impression, too. At the moment there's really nothing to distinguish it from dozens of other magazine covers on the bookstalls.' He regarded her frankly. 'Have you any suggestions as to how we might improve it?'

Of course she had! Isla smiled modestly. 'As a matter of fact, I've sketched out a couple of ideas.' She withdrew from her pile of papers the two layouts in question and laid them on the desk before him. 'Of course, they're only rough, I'm not an artist, but they give the feel of what I have in mind. I think the title should be bolder, right across the top here, instead of dangling in the corner.' She reached out to indicate what she meant. 'And we need more cover lines, just something short and punchy to catch the reader's eye.'

'I see you've changed the cover picture, too. Any particular reason for that?'

'The model was wrong for the image we're after. We want something more sophisticted. She was a bit girl-next-door.' From the tray at her elbow she picked out a couple of transparencies and, squinting, held one of them up to the light. 'I took these from the picture library, just to give an idea of the sort of thing I'm after. Here, take a look.' She handed it to Rory. 'It's much more lively than the original.'

Rory followed her example and held the transparency up to the light. 'Mmm. I see what you mean. Where would you crop it?'

Isla reached out with her pencil to demonstrate. 'Just below the necklace and about here at the top, so that the title runs across her hair.' She sat back in her seat and pulled a face. 'It's difficult to explain without the proper equipment. If we had a projector it would be easier to show you.'

'That's no problem.' Rory grinned as he slid down from the desk with a purposeful air. 'There's a projector-room just down the corridor. I sometimes use it for meetings and things.' Already, he was heading for the door. 'Come on. Let's go and do this thing properly.'

In an instant Isla was regretting having been so candid. She remained in her chair, suddenly wishing she hadn't been so thoughtless as to mention the word projector. Projector-rooms, by their very nature, tended to be dark and intimate. They were the last sort of place in which she wished to inter herself with Rory.

As he paused in the doorway, she searched for an excuse. Should she invent an appointment? Say her parents were waiting for her? For the truth was she already felt quite vulnerable enough being stuck up here alone on the third floor with him. Apart from Jackie and one or two others, the floor, indeed the building, was virtually deserted. This was the Christmas-New Year holiday and just a skeleton staff was keeping Buchanan's ticking over.

'Come on. Bring your layouts with you, and the transparencies.' Rory was still waiting in the doorway. He frowned at her curiously as she continued to hesitate. 'What's the matter? Is there some problem?'

None that he would possibly understand. He had, after all, not the faintest idea of the powerful effect he still exerted over her. If he did, all too likely, he would simply find it amusing. For what was she to him, after all, but a one-time girlfriend, long forgotten?

That thought somehow served to clarify the situation. These anxieties that were assailing her were all of her imagining. She was making a mountain out of a heap of nothing. To put it mildly, she was being plain stupid.

Smiling heroically, Isla got to her feet. 'No problem,' she assured him, gathering up her layouts. 'I was just making a mental check of what I need to bring with me.' Then on firm steps she followed him out into the corridor. In for a penny, in for a pound!

The projector room was quite as small as she had anticipated, a well-appointed room with seating for about fifty, the rows of chairs wedged tightly together, leaving only a narrow gangway down one side. As the door closed behind them, she felt a dart of claustrophobia. Maybe it was not such a good idea after all.

As she fixed one of her layouts to the screen, Rory switched on the projector for her, then seated himself in one of the front-row seats. 'It's all yours,' he told her, grinning. 'Just let me know when you're ready and I'll switch off the lights.'

Feeling unnaturally self-conscious, Isla crossed to the projector and slotted the slides into place in the carousel. She had no idea why she should be feeling so self-conscious, except that she was aware of Rory's eyes upon her, openly appraising her curvy slender form beneath the bright red figure-skimming dress she wore.

But she had felt admiring male eyes on her before. It was something she was used to. An everyday occurrence. So why should she feel a warm glow spread through her, as though his eyes had ignited her skin with their touch?

Because this whole situation is false and unnatural, she answered herself, avoiding his gaze. Because he has no right to look at me that way. In fact, he has no right to look at me at all. And if he had even a spark of decency in him he would know that for himself!

She swivelled her eyes momentarily in his direction. 'You can turn the lights out now,' she told him.

A moment later all self-consciousness had gone as she carefully focused the image on the screen into place against the layout, creating a passable representation of a front cover, and proceeded to outline her suggestions in more detail. Now she was in her element nothing could touch her, not even the execrable Rory Buchanan!

And he seemed to be in agreement with the solutions she was offering. In the reflected light of the beam from the projector she was aware of his tall figure in the front row behind her, leaning back casually in his seat, one leg hooked at the ankle over the thigh of the other, arms stretched out along the backs of the seats, the dark head nodding from time to time as he considered and approved what she was saying.

As she concluded her little monologue, his tawny gaze was on her. 'Congratulations,' he told her. 'I'm most impressed.' Then, as she met his gaze, he added softly, 'I can see why you're such a successful editor. There's no doubt you really know your stuff.'

Isla glanced away quickly, finding this personal praise almost as difficult to cope with as his earlier abuse. For she could sense it was sincere and that he had said it to please her, and she was reluctant to feel pleased on his account.

'I'm glad you approve,' she responded briskly, struggling to hide the self-consciousness she felt once more creeping up on her. With clean, efficient movements she removed the slides and switched off the projector. Then, in the sudden darkness, realising her mistake, she quickly crossed over to the light switch to turn the lights back on again.

It would have been more sensible if she had switched on the projector light first, but her brain had been momentarily fuddled and, quite uncharacteristically, she had acted without thinking. A moment later she was cursing her careless lapse as she found herself colliding head-on with Rory.

The shock of the sudden contact with him made her gasp out loud, then freeze in horror, and though she longed to pull away she felt rooted to the spot.

As his arms caught and held her, suddenly she was his prisoner, bound to him in a grip as firm as an embrace, and all she was aware of was the throbbing virility of the muscular body that held her so close. And the sensation that tore through her was no longer horror, but an anguish and a longing so fierce and so powerful it brought a tremor to her limbs and a flutter to her heart.

She could feel his warm breath caress her hair. The clean cool scent of him invaded her nostrils. And through the cool white cotton of his shirt she could sense the sweet warmth of his skin.

Isla closed her eyes as for one terrible moment she longed to sink against him as once she had done, and she had to fight back the sob that rose to her throat and the sudden tears of grief that stung in her eyes. For one deceiving instant it had seemed almost as though she were his once again and he, blessedly, hers. But then, like a mirage, the moment had vanished, leaving a sense of cold barrenness in her heart.

She snapped her eyes open as the light came on and returned to the present to hear him say, 'Two minds with but a single thought—but I beat you to it by a hair's breadth.'

He was smiling down at her, but it was a strange sort of smile, though Isla could not say why it troubled her so. It was a compassionate smile, a puzzled smile, yet with some other secret emotion flickering in the background.

He looked deep into her eyes. 'Are you all right?' he asked.

'All right? Of course I'm all right,' Isla answered, making a belated effort to wriggle free from his grip. Had he read the emotion in her eyes? she wondered. And she cursed herself for her loss of control. She tried to pull herself together. 'You just gave me a bit of a fright, that's all.'

His arms still held her, but very lightly. Had her limbs been functioning normally, she could have easily escaped. But all she had done was put an inch or two between them as he continued to look down at her with those probing tawny eyes.

Then she froze as one hand came round to touch her cheek, making her skin burn like hot coals under his touch. He leaned towards her as though he might kiss her and her mouth all at once felt as dry as a bone.

She could feel the warmth of him and hear the pounding of his heart, and the giddy scent of him poured through her senses like wine. She held her breath, like a confused and frightened rabbit, as the tawny eyes burned into hers.

For a long, perfect moment his gaze consumed her and she could see the softness and the wanting in his eyes. She could feel that old bond between them, as though it had never been broken. It reached out and curled around her soul.

Then his expression clouded. He deliberately drew back. And the distance between them felt as wide as a mile. Isla blinked in confusion as he asked her, 'Why have you gone to all this trouble with the dummy? You've done far more than you need have done, far more than I'd expected.'

What did he think? That she'd done it for him? For an instant she even wondered herself if it might be true. Then she pushed such a preposterous notion from her and informed him, 'Because I take a pride in what I'm doing. I like to do things properly. No other reason.'

His eyes were still clouded. 'Yes, I remember. In matters pertaining to work you were always most conscientious.' He paused and sighed, speaking volumes without words, managing to suggest with perfect eloquence that he considered this to be more of a minus than a plus. Then, before she could speak, he went on to astound her by enquiring in an oddly matter-of-fact voice, 'How come you've never married, Isla? A beautiful, desirable girl like you.'

For a moment Isla simply blinked at him. What right did he of all people have to ask her that? She looked back at him with hostile violet eyes. 'Maybe I have no desire to get married!' she countered. 'Maybe I'm quite happy with my career.'

Rory nodded. 'Yes. I suppose that's the answer. Though I can't help thinking it's something of a waste.'

Isla longed to back away from him, to widen the physical gap between them, but she had become wedged between him and a row of seats and there was no place for her to move to. She straightened and glared at him. 'Well, I don't want your opinion. My personal life is none of your damned business.' She narrowed her eyes and elaborated further, 'In fact, I'm frankly surprised you give it a second thought.'

'Of course I do. I haven't forgotten. I can remember the passionate young woman behind the career girl and I've a feeling she still exists. Or she would if only you'd give her a chance.'

That did it! Now he had gone too far! The confusion that had been immobilising her suddenly hardened to hostile anger. Her voice was brittle as she put to him, 'Does your wife know you go in for these intimate scenarios with old girlfriends? Do you think she'd approve of your behaviour right now? Personally, I find it somewhat inappropriate for a married man.'

A shutter seemed to drop down over his eyes, reminding her of that time at Kirkhaven Castle when her mention of his wife had brought a similar response. Then he pursed his lips and leaned back against the wall, folding his arms across his chest, saying nothing, just continuing to stare at her with those deeply unsettling tawny eyes, and she could sense there was a battle going on inside him.

Then he pulled himself upright and dropped his arms to his sides, and in a strange tone of voice, half earnest, half throw-away, he informed her, 'I'm not sure I can be classified as a married man. You see, I have no marriage. I have no wife.'

An alarm bell sounded in Isla's head. She had heard this kind of claim before. 'Are you trying to tell me,' she queried frankly, 'that that woman you live with is a figment of everyone's imagination?'

A smile touched his lips, fleeting and cynical. He stuffed his hands into his trouser pockets. 'Oh, no, she's real enough,' he answered. 'But we have no marriage any more. We may appear to live together, but we are really like strangers.'

It was Isla's turn now for a cynical smile. 'I understand.' Her tone was damning. 'Though I can't say as a line it's very original. I would have thought you were capable of better than that.'

The fact was it was more or less word for word the very same line that James had spun her that day she had confronted him with her discovery that he had a wife and child in Belsize Park. It was the pathetic, well-worn anthem of the philandering married man. I have no marriage. My wife doesn't understand me.

Something shrivelled within her as she looked into Rory's face. That James should stoop so low as to try to justify his behaviour with such a threadbare and blatantly deceitful excuse was already quite bad enough. James, she had discovered belatedly, was weak and unprincipled. But that Rory should do likewise was deeply shocking. She had believed he had more character, in spite of all his faults.

He was still watching her with that guarded expression in his eyes, as though he was carefully assessing her reaction. As she sensed he was about to enlarge on his deception Isla finally dislodged herself from the corner in which he had trapped her and swung away from him down the narrow gangway. Over her shoulder she advised him, 'Kindly don't waste your breath by enlightening me further! I don't want to hear another word about your damned marriage! You can absolutely take my word for it I couldn't be less interested in your private affairs.'

He had remained standing exactly where she had left him, by the row of light switches at the end of the gangway, his hands thrust into the pockets of his trousers, his shoulders leaning lightly against the wall. He raised one dark eyebrow at her and shrugged. 'Suit yourself,' he told her mildly.

'Damned right I'll suit myself.' Isla rounded on him angrily. 'Don't think that journalism is the only thing I've learned over the past eight years down in London. I've learnt a thing or two about men as well—which is perhaps why I prefer to stick to the former! So, just in case you were thinking of trying to talk me into a little something extra "for old times' sake", as you might put it, you can forget that idea right this minute!'

She swung away in fury to the projector and snatched the cover transparencies from the carousel, then grabbed the layout from the projector screen and thrust it angrily under her arm. She was heading for the door on the stiff legs of outrage when, suddenly, he stepped out into her path.

'Quite a performance.' His tone was mocking and there was a sudden hard look in his eyes. 'But, don't worry, I wasn't planning anything—not for old times' sake or anything else. If I was looking for a bit of fun on the side, you can rest assured my last choice would be you.'

The golden eagle eyes looked into hers to ensure she had fully absorbed the insult, then he stepped aside to allow her passage and added to her hostile, retreating back, 'You're wise to stick to your editing, Isla. It's the only damned thing you're any good at.'

CHAPTER SIX

THAT evening Isla took a taxi home, icily declining Rory's offer of a lift.

'I have some shopping to do in town,' she offered defensively when he raised one questioning dark eyebrow at her. 'It's better if I make my own arrangements.'

He stood in the doorway of her office and shrugged broad shoulders in response. 'Suit yourself. It's all the same to me.' He made to leave. 'I'll see you tomorrow.'

'I'm afraid I won't be coming in tomorrow. I'll take some stuff home with me and work from there.'

'I see.' He smiled in cynical understanding, and for a moment Isla thought he was about to say more. But at the very last moment he changed his mind. He turned on his heel. 'Then I'll see you when I see you.'

As the door closed behind him, Isla slumped back in her chair, feeling the tension in her finally ebb a little. I'll see you when I see you, he had said. If she had her way, that would be never.

Quickly, she gathered up her things, including the layouts and piles of notes she had made, and stuffed them into a plastic bag. She had been a fool to risk tangling with Rory again. She might have known it would only lead to pain. She had thought she was long over him, and in a way she was, but only in the same precarious way that an alcoholic was ever cured. As long as she stayed away from him her heart was safe. But if she allowed herself to take one taste, she would be halfway down the road to ruin.

She got up from her desk and pulled her coat down from the hanger at the back of the door. It was not, of course, that she was still in love with him. Her love had long ago turned to hate. But, nevertheless, there was still something about him, some irresistible power that drew her to him. Perhaps in her heart she had always known that, and that was why she had avoided him all those years. She should never have risked exposing herself to him so freely. She ought to have known how it would end.

She buttoned her coat and turned up the collar, then slung her tan shoulder-bag over her shoulder. Then, making a quick check that she had forgotten nothing, she grabbed the plastic bag and headed for the door. This time it was goodbye Buchanan's forever. She would never walk through these doors again.

It was only as she stepped out on to the pavement and breathed in a lungful of the clean, frosty air that Isla allowed her mind to focus briefly on that moment of near-intimacy in the projector-room that had led to this surge of panic in her soul.

Naïvely, she had believed that Rory had no idea of the disruptive effect he still exerted over her. But from that look in his eyes as he had stood there holding her, supposedly saving her from a collision, he was, contrarily, only too well aware—and, apparently, cynically eager to exploit her weakness.

He had been a heartbeat away from trying to kiss her and she had been too paralysed to move.

The thought made her shudder. Lord, the man was married! And after what he had done to her, how could she have just stood there like some meek and helpless thing?

She walked briskly into the snowflakes that had started falling, her knuckles white around the handle of her plastic carrier. That was why she would be making no more visits to his office. She would finish to her satisfaction the work she was doing, then find a way to get the files and things back to him.

But, as far as she and Rory were concerned, their paths must never cross again.

Next day was the last day of the year. A day for exorcising ghosts and looking to the future. And since nowhere in the world was Hogmanay celebrated more enthusiastically than it was in Scotland, Isla was determined to enter into the spirit of things.

It was her parents who had talked her into joining the McLarens for the celebrations at Glenshee. 'You'll have a much better time with people your own age than you will staying at home with two old fogies like your dad and me.'

'Go on, girl. Enjoy yourself,' Bill MacDonald had insisted, backing up his wife, as always. 'We'll be seeing the New Year in with a couple of the neighbours. Don't worry about us. You go to the party.'

And so, in the end, Isla had agreed. She had been friendly with the McLarens since childhood. Their family cottage was just down the road from her parents' and Eck McLaren, the father, was the local blacksmith. Jean and Hamish, the eldest son and daughter, were now married with their own homes in Strathallane, but they were a close family and, just as when they were children, they still enjoyed doing things together. So Jean and Hamish, along with their spouses and their younger brother, Andrew, who still lived at home, were all going together to the Hogmanay party at the Drumlaggan Hotel up in Glenshee.

'Bring your pyjamas,' Andrew had warned her when she went to break the news that she was accepting their invitation. 'We're staying overnight. It's better that way. It's a bit of a drive back and the roads could be bad.'

Isla had laughed. 'Not to mention the drivers! I doubt any of you will be in a fit state even to think about driving!'

'I certainly hope not!' Andrew had laughed with her. 'It wouldn't be much of a Hogmanay if any of us were still sober at the end of it!'

The six of them set off in Hamish's Volvo just a little after five o'clock. The plan was to get to their hotel in plenty of time to settle into their rooms and change for dinner. And although it was only a fifty-mile drive to Glenshee, the road in winter could be notoriously bad, and a lot of snow had fallen and more was forecast. It was wise to give themselves plenty of time.

Wedged in the back seat between Jean and Carol, Hamish's wife, Isla looked out at the snowy landscape and felt the tension within her fade away. It had been an inspired idea to accept the invitation of this friendly group of people whom she knew so well. In their company she felt carefree, almost a child again, and with them she could relax as with few others she knew.

For to the McLarens she was simply young Isla MacDonald, the pigtailed girl they'd climbed trees with in the woods and gone strawberry picking with in the summer holidays. The fact that she was now a high-powered London editor had never for one moment affected the way they treated her, and for that Isla had always been immensely grateful.

Inwardly she sighed. How could it be that these simple people could see that beneath the veneer of sophistication she was still the same old Isla as before when in the eyes of Rory, who should be more perceptive, she had apparently turned into something quite despicable?

She pushed the thought away as, for a moment, it threatened to cast a dark shadow over her mood. She must not think of him. She must cast him from her. As the old year would be shed tonight at midnight, so must he be shed from her life forever.

Glenshee had a well-deserved reputation for being one of the most picturesque of the Scottish glens. As they came through Blairgowrie then headed north by Dalrulzian, rugged mountains on all sides dressed in vivid winter-white, Isla peered through the darkness, feeling a lump in her throat. It was here that as a child she had learned to ski. The memories and the beauty of it took her breath away.

Drumlaggan Hotel was an old country house, impeccably run by a local family—all carved wooden staircases, meandering corridors, old oak beams and open wood fires. And when the Volvo drew up outside the front door, just a little before seven, the place was already a hive of activity. Tonight, undoubtedly, would be the busiest night of their year!

A plump, smiling woman showed them to their rooms. 'Our special dinner starts at nine this evening. A table has been reserved for you,' she told them. Then she added with an apologetic smile at Isla, 'I hope you don't mind sleeping in the little attic-room? I'm afraid it was the only room we had left.'

Isla shook her head. 'I don't mind in the slightest. I'm sure the attic-room is just perfect.'

And indeed it was, tiny but exquisite, with its brass bed and pretty floral curtains and magnificent view out over the glen. Isla unpacked the dress she had brought for the party and laid it out carefully on the bed. This place was delightful. A positive tonic. And an omen, she thought positively, for the year ahead.

Half an hour later she was ready to meet the others downstairs in the bar. Wrapping her stole around her shoulders, she glanced quickly in the mirror, a smile of pleasure and approval curving round her lips. In the plaid green taffeta with its full rustling skirt, demure scoop neckline and cinched-in waist she looked five years younger, almost girlish, an impression reinforced by her excited rosy cheeks and the sparkle of anticipation in the bright violet eyes, from which all trace of a shadow had temporarily vanished.

She shook back her glossy chestnut bob and adjusted the straps of her spindly gold sandals. Tonight she was really going to enjoy herself. Nothing could stand in the way of that.

Downstairs things were fast moving into gear. The huge dining-room had been turned into a dining-room-cum-ballroom with a Scottish country dance band already playing in one corner. There was a lilt in the air that was reflected in the smiles of the patrons already crowded in the bar. On Hogmanay everyone was everyone's friend, and everyone wanted to buy his friend a drink.

Their own little group was as merry as any as they chatted and laughed about this and that.

'I'll bet they don't have New Year parties like this down in England,' Hamish teased her as the band next door struck up with a reel.

And Isla laughed, in no position to contradict him. 'I'd forgotten just how much fun these things can be.'

Andrew nudged her. 'And we haven't even started yet!'

By the time they all moved into the dining-room, whose every pillar and chandelier was festooned with bunches of holly and mistletoe and hundreds of multi-coloured balloons, the atmosphere was decidedly jolly. They found their table—with a good view of the dance-floor—ordered wine and waited for the party to begin.

But it was just as the waiter was serving their starter, pheasant pâté served with curly Melba toast, that Isla caught sight, from the corner of her eye, of a vision that sent her poor heart thumping through the floor.

Rory Buchanan, resplendent in a black suit, sitting just a couple of tables away.

He had seen her, of course. He was looking straight at her. He even had the gall to raise his glass and wink at her before turning away with a mocking little smile to bestow his attention once more on his friends.

Isla's immediate instinct was to get up from the table, go to her room and pack her bag, then take the first available taxi home. And had it not been for the need to consider her friends, she might very well in fact have done so. For there was really not a great deal of point in her staying. The evening was a write-off before it had begun. And it had never even crossed her mind for an instant that Rory might be here.

'Isla, are you all right?'

Suddenly a cool hand touched her arm and she jerked round to find Jean frowning into her eyes. 'Isla, are you OK?' she repeated. 'You suddenly looked a little pale.'

Isla pulled herself together. 'I'm fine, thanks,' she answered. 'I think it must be hunger. I haven't eaten all day.' She grabbed her cutlery and made a valiant show of attacking her pâté, but the truth was her appetite had suddenly vanished—thanks to the black-suited man just two tables away.

A brief glance told her that she was not acquainted with any of the people he was with. Another one confirmed that Evelyn was not among them, which seemed more than a little strange on Hogmanay. Perhaps there was some truth in that story he had told her about the parlous state of his marriage. After all, she remembered, his wife hadn't even accompanied him to the midnight service on Christmas Eve. Maybe, as he had said, they really did live like strangers.

Isla checked herself instantly. All that was immaterial. None of it in any way changed the situation. Whether happily or unhappily, he was still married, and, whether or not she liked it, he was still here.

The only solution, she decided, was to ignore him, just to concentrate her attention on the group she was with and exclude all thoughts of him from her head. Otherwise the evening would be a total disaster.

This remedy proved less than easy in practice. Rory was not an easy man to ignore. Somehow, entirely against her will, Isla's eyes kept drifting across to his table, to the dark sculpted profile with its slightly crooked nose and head of glossy raven-dark hair, so that she had to keep snatching them away. And once the dancing began, his tall manly figure seemed effortlessly to dominate the floor, making it almost impossible not to glance his way.

He danced frequently, she noticed, and as gracefully as ever, but never with the same partner twice. Perhaps his wife was ill, she conjectured privately, and this was a perfectly respectable evening out with friends. Whatever the situation, his comportment was impeccable.

Of course the evening, for Isla, had lost its sparkle. Rory's presence was like a dead weight in her chest. But, thanks to her friends, she managed to enjoy herself. It was not a total write-off, after all.

As they danced and laughed and joked together, the hour of midnight was fast approaching and the excitement in the hall was tightening like a bow.

'Let's go out and watch the skiers,' Hamish suggested. 'They'll be coming down the mountain on the stroke of twelve.'

'Oh, let's! I'd love to!' Isla was enthusiastic, for she had never seen the midnight skiers before.

'They come down the mountainside carrying torches,' Andrew had explained to her earlier in the evening. 'It's really quite spectacular. A fabulous sight.'

But the two wives were reluctant. 'It's cold out there!' Jean protested. 'And besides,' echoed the other, 'we've seen it before.'

So, in the end, it was only Isla and Andrew who decided to brave the elements and watch the show. 'I'll see you down in the lobby,' Andrew told her, as the two of them dashed upstairs to get their coats.

Five minutes later Isla was hurrying back down again, her navy cashmere coat slung loosely about her shoulders, and, though the lobby was crowded with scores of others making their way outside to watch the midnight skiers, there was no sign of Andrew anywhere.

Isla glanced at her watch. It was ten minutes to midnight. There wasn't much time left to get outside and find a good spot from which to watch the spectacle. A sudden thought occurred to her. Perhaps she had misunderstood and Andrew had said for them to meet outside. She made a final thorough check of the lobby and decided that must be the case.

She pulled her coat around her and hurried outside to where the throng of noisy, excited guests were gathering in groups around the perimeter of the forecourt, all heads turned towards the towering

mountain that stood over them like a silent, be-
nevolent protector, its snowy slopes illuminated by
a battery of floodlamps.

Someone had thrown open the windows of the
dance hall and the clear frosty air all about them
was filled with the music of a dozen Scottish fid-
dlers. Isla smiled to herself as she hurried down to
the forecourt, feeling her previous claustrophobia
dissolve away like magic. It felt good to be free of
Rory's oppressive presence. Out here in the open
she could breathe again.

She had barely gone two steps, however, when
she paused to curse herself for not having had the
foresight to change her footwear. Away from the
path the snow was deep and her spindly gold sandals
were no protection at all. They weren't even
particularly easy to walk in, she conceded ruefully
as she picked her way. Any minute she was liable
to go over on her ankle and end up in a heap in
the snow!

A hand touched her arm. 'Allow me to help you.'
And without even thinking, assuming it was
Andrew, Isla leaned gratefully on a strong male
arm.

'I thought I'd lost you!' She turned to greet him
and felt the smile on her face crack instantly at the
corners. *'You!'* she gasped, meeting a pair of tawny
eyes. 'What the devil are *you* doing here?'

'The same as you. I've come to see the skiers.'
As she snatched her arm away Rory glanced down
at her sandals. 'But you're not going to get very
far in these.'

Isla made an effort to stride womanfully in front
of him. 'I can manage!' she fumed in irritation,

unsuccessfuly striving to disguise the fact that her scantily clad foot had just sunk up to the ankle in a drift of crunchy white snow.

Rory laughed. 'Sure you can!' he teased. 'But not in time to see the skiers come down.'

As he glanced at his watch, Isla did likewise and frowned as she noted it was now four minutes to twelve. At this rate she might make it in time for *next* year, but this year's spectacle was in danger of passing her by.

Rory, evidently, was of the very same opinion. 'Come on,' he instructed, and then without further ado he had caught her lightly by the waist and was scooping her effortlessly up into his arms.

'Put me down this very minute!' Isla kicked her legs and struggled for dear life, her fists pounding the hard shoulders with all her might. 'Didn't you hear me? I said put me down! How dare you take such a liberty with me?'

Mid-stride, he paused and looked into her eyes. 'I'll put you down if you really want me to.' And he extended his arms as though with the intention of dropping her writhing body straight into the snow.

Isla grew still. 'You wouldn't!' she challenged, though she was decidedly less than a hundred per cent sure.

His eyes were still on her, their expression ambiguous, though a spark of amusement lit their dark tawny depths. 'Not if you behave yourself I won't. It's entirely up to you.'

Isla dropped her eyes away from his as he proceeded to carry her across the snow, and contented herself with a quiet grumble. 'I really can't see why you're bothering. This Sir Galahad act is most unlike you.'

'Is it?' He raised one shapely black eyebrow. 'I always thought it was one of my more endearing characteristics that I like to rescue damsels in distress.' He caught her eye and held it. 'Surely you can't have forgotten? Gallantry is my middle name.'

Isla glanced away. She had not forgotten. Nor had she forgotten that it was she who had first said that about gallantry being his middle name. In those long ago days, before she really knew him, she had always been impressed by his chivalrous ways.

'Besides,' he was saying, 'gallantry apart, it's surely the very least I could do for an old friend.'

Isla pursed her lips and refrained from replying. His easy references to their former relationship never failed to send a stab of anger through her heart. And she sensed he knew it, which was why he did it. He derived endless amusement in trying to undermine her.

They had reached the edge of the crowd down in the forecourt, all jostling now for the perfect view. 'You can put me down now,' Isla commanded. 'I've arranged to meet a friend of mine.'

'He's not here,' Rory told her, as he kept right on going. 'So you're coming with me, and kindly don't protest.' And on long strides he proceeded past the body of the onlookers. 'We'll have a much better view from this end, I assure you, with a measure of privacy as an additional bonus.'

Isla felt almost as though she were being borne off by some gigantic bird of prey as he kept on going to the end of the forecourt, then round a corner and down some stone steps. But at least he had been right about Andrew not being there, for she had scoured every face as they'd hurried on past. In the circumstances, she decided philosophically, there seemed little point in making a fuss.

At last they reached the spot that he was aiming for, and before setting her down carefully on the ground he kicked away the snow with his foot. 'You see,' he told her, grinning, as she adjusted her coat, 'this Sir Galahad stuff seems to be in my blood.'

Isla smiled thinly. 'Yes,' she agreed with sarcasm. 'It's all a part of your natural, irresistible charm.'

Pulling up her coat collar, she looked around her. The spot where he had brought her, as he had promised, was private, out of sight of the other spectators and with a wonderful view of the glistening ski slopes. And in spite of herself, through a shaft of uneasiness at their solitude, she couldn't stop herself from smiling.

This was so typical of the Rory she had once known, full of surprises, always out of the ordinary, forever with an ace hidden up his sleeve. And for an instant she had a rush of the old warm excitement she always used to feel when they were together, an excitement she hadn't felt for years.

He had this knack of making every event extraspecial, an almost childlike enthusiasm for everything he did that he passed on, like chicken-pox, to whomever he was with. Most people showed you the world as it was—drab or serious, tragic or droll. But with Rory you could believe there was a man in the moon, that the clouds were pink candy-floss and the stars fairies' wands.

She had forgotten how real his magic could be. The rediscovery lit a glow of sudden optimism inside.

'Hey, look up there!' His arm was round her as he bade her follow his pointing finger. And there, sure enough, at the top of the mountain, she caught a fleeting, flickering glimpse of a glowing red torch.

Above them, the crowd had begun the countdown in unison—'Ten! Nine! Eight!'—and the air was pulsing with excitement. Even the music in the background had temporarily stopped as the whole world waited for the magic hour of midnight.

The skiers on the mountainside were more visible now. At least, the flares of their torches could be clearly seen as they zigzagged gracefully down the side of the mountain. The skiers themselves, dressed all in white, could scarcely be distinguished from the endless snowy background.

The crowd was still chanting. 'Seven! Six!' And Isla was aware, as the tension mounted, of Rory's arm slipping round her waist.

She did not want to dislodge it. It felt oddly right there. She loved the warm familiar feel of it. And that, she rebuked herself with a pang of horror, was all the more reason why she must not allow it to remain there.

Deliberately she slid away from him and, firmly and pointedly, removed the offending arm. 'I can stand quite well without support,' she told him crisply. 'I'd prefer you to keep your hands to yourself.'

He made a gesture of amused repentance. 'What's the matter, Isla, don't you like to be touched? I don't remember you having any such hang-ups before.'

Isla turned away from him, not daring to look at him, aware of a sharp shaft of anguish in her heart. They were far too secluded here, far too private. It would be far too easy, knowing that no one could see them, to succumb to the longing that twisted inside her. For though it shamed her to admit it, even privately, far from finding the touch of him unpleasant, she was suddenly filled with a dark and painful yearning to feel his arm slip round her again.

She crushed the unworthy longing like an insect and, with an effort, focused her attention on the mountain and the moving snake of skiers with their torches held aloft as they came more clearly into view. Dimly, she was aware of Rory saying, 'Only another couple of seconds to go.'

The chanting behind them was growing louder— 'Four! Three! Two!'—filling the air around them with jubilant excitement.

Rory smiled across at her. 'The old year is over.' And an instant later the crowd erupted, and from the hotel could be heard the sudden uproar as the band broke into 'Auld Lang Syne'.

It was a moment of exquisite pain and happiness. For an instant the past and the present were mingled, the dividing line between the two broken. In an instant she was swept back to that very first New Year that she and Rory had welcomed in together, and for a moment all the hopes and expectations that had burned within her so brightly then flared foolishly inside her again.

She could have wept for the beauty and the bitterness of those memories, as Rory leaned towards her now and murmured, 'Isla, Happy New Year!'

Isla took a deep breath. 'Happy New Year,' she offered. She could not bear to look into his face.

'Is that it?' He was smiling down at her. 'Don't I even get a New Year's kiss?'

As he spoke he had reached out to touch her cheek. His fingers were like fire against her skin. And all at once her heart had stilled within her. Her feet were stuck like limpets to the ground.

'Surely an old friend can claim a New Year's kiss?' His fingers were sliding into her hair. 'You wouldn't be so cruel as to deny me that, surely?'

It was he who was being cruel, if only he knew it. His touch tormented her like a torturer's pincers. The warmth of his fingers against her skin tore at her senses without pity. The pain was so fierce she felt it must kill her.

She raised her eyes to him in supplication, knowing she had not the strength to speak. But already, mercilessly, he was leaning towards her.

In that instant before his lips met hers a thousand and one thoughts went rushing through her head.

Surely there could be no harm in a friendly little kiss? After all, it was Hogmanay. Everyone exchanged kisses on Hogmanay! A Hogmanay kiss meant nothing at all!

But this was to be no Hogmanay kiss. She could see the dark glint in his eyes, feel the way his hand had tautened in her hair, sense the heat that burned within him.

As his mouth touched hers, his lips pressing too firmly, his warm tongue already threatening to invade her, with all her strength Isla tore herself free. This man who was presuming to behave so intimately was a man she hated, a man who had betrayed her. And a man who, most significantly of all, happened to be married to another woman.

She pounded him with her fists. 'What do you think you're doing?' Then, as he blinked down at her with startled eyes, she was pushing her way past him up the stone steps to the forecourt where, earlier, the crowd had been gathered.

She was relieved to see that there was no longer anyone there, though a few couples could still be seen, further off, drifting back towards the hotel.

Oblivious of her sandals she stumbled through the snow, ignoring Rory's cries of 'Isla! Isla!' All she wanted was to get back to her friends, away from Rory, back to sanity.

But he was right behind her and all of a sudden he was stretching out and catching her by the arm. 'Isla, wait! I've something to tell you. Isla, for heaven's sake, give me a chance.'

As she wrenched her arm free from his, she staggered and fell, landing face first in the powder-soft snow. But even as he reached out to help to her feet, she was scrabbling away from him and yelling like a banshee, 'Leave me alone! You had your chance! You'll never get another one! So, just get out of my life!'

Then she was back on her feet and racing clumsily towards the hotel, leaving the lone black-suited figure far behind her, a dark, unmoving silhouette against the silent, brooding backcloth of the snow-white mountain.

CHAPTER SEVEN

'I THINK I'll leave the day after tomorrow, if I can get a seat on the train.'

Isla was in the kitchen with her mother as they prepared a light tea for New Year's Day. She kept her eyes on the Dundee cake she was slicing, carefully avoiding looking at her mother. The look of disappointment on the older woman's face might have persuaded her to stay on a day or two longer, and she knew in her heart it was time for her to leave.

She had got home from Glenshee just after lunchtime, her mind already made up about her departure. It had been made up since last night when she had struggled across the snow, desperately fleeing from Rory's advances. For mingled with the fury she had felt against him, and the almost equal fury she had felt against herself for allowing herself to be led on like that, was the rock-hard, iron-clad resolution that there must be no repetition.

And there was only one way to ensure that. She must leave. Immediately.

On awakening this morning after a semi-sleepless night endlessly haunted by her old nightmare, Isla had been doubly certain. She had come to Scotland in search of tranquillity, but all she had found was even more heartache. The sooner she was gone, the better.

'We'll be sorry to see you go, but it's been wonderful having you.' Isobel MacDonald smiled at her daughter. 'I hope it won't be too long before we see you again.'

'Definitely not,' Isla assured her, grateful that in spite of her obvious feelings of sadness her mother wasn't trying to persuade her to stay on. She reached across and patted her hand affectionately. 'I promise I'll be back again before next Christmas.'

The promise inevitably made her think of Rory. Rory who, once again, was the cause of her flight. She *would* come back, she would not break her promise, although she would be scrupulously careful in the future never to cross his path again.

As to the business of Jock Campbell's field, she would simply have to trust to his integrity. She had more than fulfilled her side of the bargain with the work she'd done for the new magazine—something that Rory had more or less admitted. But if, in spite of that, he chose to go ahead with the building, she would simply have to find some other way to stop him. Some way that involved negotiation through a third party. For she would have no personal dealings with him ever again.

She glanced across at her mother. 'You'll let me know at once if there are any developments regarding Jock Campbell's field. Let's just keep our fingers crossed that there'll be none.'

'I'm sure there won't be. I'm sure we're safe now.' Isobel MacDonald sounded a great deal more confident than her daughter felt. 'After all that work you've done for Rory, how could he go back on his word?' She shook her head. 'He wouldn't do a thing like that.'

'Let's hope not.' Isla kept her doubts to herself. There was no point in puncturing her mother's optimism when, after all, she might be right. But the fact, of course, was that Rory had promised nothing. He couldn't go back on his word because he had never given it.

She stole a glance at her mother as she prepared the tea tray with scones and Dundee cake and juicy Black Bun. She had, of course, told her nothing about what had passed—or *almost* passed—between herself and Rory last night. She had not even told her he'd been at the party. And as she prepared to carry the tea-tray through to the sitting-room she couldn't help surmising that her mother's lofty opinion of Rory would be seriously undermined if she were ever to find out.

Foolish, thought Isla with a stab of bitterness. If she but knew it, with a few exceptions, married men were all alike!

At the thought a cold hand closed around her heart. Dealing with James, her first experience of the breed, had been a relatively easy, pain-free experience. But resisting Rory's kiss last night had been like wrenching her poor, bleeding heart from her bosom. She had wanted him. She could not deny it. Thank heavens she had found the strength to say no.

Now that she had made the decision to return to London there was one small problem Isla had to solve. How was she to get the dummy and all the files she had brought home with her back to Rory before she left? The Buchanan building would be closed until the day of her departure and, since she planned to leave early in the morning, it would be impossible to hand it in then.

Of course, she could always leave the chore to her parents. They'd even offered when she'd brought the subject up. But she was loath to impose on them; it would put them out. And, besides, she disliked the idea of leaving without all the loose ends being tied up. Somehow she had to get the files and things back to Rory before she actually left.

'Take them to the house,' her mother had suggested. 'I'm sure he wouldn't mind a bit.'

But Isla, quite naturally, had balked at that idea. It did not appeal to her in the slightest. And yet, though she thought and thought, she could come up with no alternative. It was beginning to look as though she didn't have much choice.

Maybe they'll be out, she told herself hopefully, as the following day, just after lunchtime, she borrowed her parents' little Renault and set off reluctantly for the Buchanan mansion. Then she could simply leave the files in some safe place and pop an explanatory note through the front door. Considering the season, she might well be lucky. New Year in Scotland was a time for visiting relatives and friends.

Greystanes, the Buchanan mansion, stood high up on a hill with a breathtaking view out over Strathallane and the magnificent snow-clad Grampians to the west. It was a house that had been built in the early nineteenth century, at the peak of the Industrial Revolution, and its classic style, based on the old baronial castles, gave it an air of grandeur and importance.

It had been in the hands of the Buchanans for over a century and had been taken over by Rory six years ago at the time of his marriage to Evelyn McDiarmid, when his mother, Elizabeth, had discreetly moved out to the luxurious granny house at the other end of the estate.

Isla approached it now with some trepidation, a state of mind remarkably similar to the one in which she had approached it eight years ago on her one and only previous visit. Then she had been worried about meeting Rory's mother, an apprehension which, in the event, had proved to be remarkably well-founded. She and Elizabeth had disliked one another on sight.

Ironically, now what filled her with anxiety was the thought of having to come face to face, not with the mother, but with the son, whom all those years ago she had believed she would marry.

Her fingers were tight around the steering-wheel as she drove through the gates with their mounted stone eagles, then up the elegant wide curved driveway flanked on either side by snow-sprinkled plane trees. She would leave the car a little way from the house, she had decided, and walk the rest of the way on foot. It would allow her to see before being seen, though she was unsure what advantage that might give her. All she knew was that she was going to need every advantage she could give herself.

She parked the car in a shady corner and paused to examine her face in the rear-view mirror. She looked strained, she decided; there was a furrow between her brows and her full, soft mouth was tight at the corners.

All thanks to Rory, she told herself resentfully, smoothing back her sleek, bobbed hair. She could always count on him to screw up her life!

With a flash of anger she gathered up the files in their protective plastic bag, grabbed her tan shoulder-bag and reached for the door-handle. Thank heavens that once this last ordeal was over there would be no more Rory to mess up her life. No more Rory ever again.

She climbed out and turned up the collar of her coat, then clutching the handles of the plastic carrier bag she headed on brisk strides for the house. Suddenly she was anxious to get the whole thing over with. With this mission would end a dark chapter of her life.

The house came into view quite suddenly as she rounded a bend at the end of the driveway, and she paused in her tracks just for a moment in order to get her bearings. Should she go to the main door? she wondered momentarily, eyeing the imposing stone-carved entrance with its magnificent brass-studded door. Or would it be wiser to opt for the back door in the hope that she might be able to offload her delivery on some servant without the need to face either the master or the mistress of the house?

The front door, she decided, stepping forward. Her visit, after all, was perfectly legitimate. She had no need to skulk.

But it was that momentary pause that caused her eye to fall on the conservatory at the side of the house, and even as she started heading for the front door a figure beyond the glass panes had caught her attention.

A woman, apparently quite oblivious of her presence, was absorbed in the pruning of some plants. A woman she instantly recognised as Evelyn, Rory's supposedly estranged wife. And suddenly, as she stared at her, Isla could not move and she was aware of a sick sensation in her throat.

For in a flash she understood why Evelyn had not been present at the watch-night service on Christmas Eve, nor at the Hogmanay festivities at Glenshee. But it was nothing to do with what Rory had told her—all those lies about how they lived like strangers, about how their marriage was no marriage any more.

For the woman in the conservatory, Isla could see quite plainly, was heavily pregnant, close to term. The reason Evelyn had not been seen in public recently was because she was about to give birth at any moment to Rory's baby.

For a moment Isla simply gaped in horror, aware that the thing she had most dreaded happening had finally come to pass. She felt illogical tears start way back in her eyes as a flood of bitter memories all at once came tumbling back on her. That child that lay protected now in Evelyn's womb was the child that, once, she had dreamed might be hers.

The handles of the carrier bag were biting into her fingers. She glanced down at the bulging contents, hours of honest toil, and suddenly she hated Rory with all her strength for his blatant, cynical dishonesty.

'Damn you!' she muttered under her breath. 'Damn you, Rory Buchanan, straight to hell—and thank heaven I'll be rid of you tomorrow!'

She almost didn't hear the car approaching. In her grief and her anger it was almost upon her before she caught the crunch of the tyres on the gravel. With a start she spun round to see the silver-grey Jaguar, with Rory at the wheel, almost upon her.

For a moment she just stood there, paralysed to the spot, then in a gesture more eloquent than any words she flung the bulging carrier bag beneath the Jaguar's wheels.

Instantly, the big car skidded to a halt. Then the window slid down and an angry-faced Rory leaned out to yell, 'Have you taken leave of your senses? What the hell do you think you're doing?'

She turned on him. 'I'm returning your files to you, you bastard! Only I wish I'd thrown them in the river!'

She saw him frown, but already she was running past him, escaping down the driveway, heading for her car. Let him speculate all he liked as to the cause of her outburst. Never in a million years would he know!

Isla reached the Renault feeling faint and breathless, her limbs trembling like jellies from that outburst of emotion. But somehow she managed to haul open the door, collapse inside and jam the key in the ignition. The next instant, with a noisy crash of gears, she was executing a haphazard three-point turn. Then, through the mist of angry tears in her eyes, barely aware of where she was going, she was heading in a rapid but wobbly line through the main gates and out on to the road.

She had barely covered two hundred yards when, through the rear-view mirror, she caught sight of the Jaguar coming up fast behind her. She jammed the accelerator into the floorboards and cursed again beneath her breath. Why the devil was he following her? What deceit and evil was he up to now?

He was gaining so fast she seemed to be going backwards, yet she was stamping so hard now on the accelerator she could hear the Renault's engine whine with the strain. But it was an unequal contest. She didn't stand a chance. The mighty Jaguar with all that power beneath its bonnet could have devoured a dozen little Renaults and spat out the pips without making a gear change. She felt her heart sink as it came alongside her, and above the revving of the engine she could just make out Rory yelling at her to stop.

'I'll be damned if I will!' she muttered back without looking at him. 'If you want me to stop, you'll have to make me!'

Two seconds later it was almost as though he had lip-read, and accepted, her challenge. With an arrogant growl the Jaguar overtook her and rapidly put a few hundred metres between them. Then, even as she was wondering if he had tired of the game and was mercifully about to drive off and leave her, the big car slewed neatly across the road, forming a barrier right in her path.

Instantly her foot was on the brake, bringing the little car to a juddering halt just a matter of a few feet away. Trembling with fury, she wound down her window, just as he climbed out and strode towards her. 'That was a bloody silly thing to do!' she screeched. 'I could easily have gone straight into you!'

He ignored her protest and, before she could stop him, he snatched open her door and stood towering over her. 'Get out!' he told her, his face like thunder.

Isla blinked up at him. Had he gone crazy? 'I'll damned well do nothing of the kind!' she informed him.

'You'll either get out or I'll haul you out. The choice is yours. I'll count to three.' He started counting.

He could not be serious, Isla told herself in panic, her eyes darting quickly up and down the road, praying to see some approaching vehicle. But in both directions the road was empty. It looked as though no one would be coming to her aid.

'Three!' He finished counting, his eyes narrowed as he glared down at her. 'I'll give you one last chance to get out under your own steam. Otherwise, I'm afraid, I shall have to keep my promise.'

There was no way Isla was going to be bullied into obeying him. She made a futile effort to grab her door shut. 'Just leave me alone! I want nothing to do with you!'

'That's just too bad!' He took a step towards her. 'We have unfinished business, you and I.'

Then to her astounded horror—she had not really believed he would do it—he was reaching across to release her seatbelt, then grabbing her firmly by the arm to drag her bodily out of the car, the entire exercise performed with the ease of a gourmet liberating an oyster from its shell.

Still holding her tightly, he reached inside and with his free hand retrieved her bag, then a moment later, shoving the bag at her, he slammed the door shut and proceeded to propel her towards the Jaguar.

'Where the hell do you think you're taking me?' Isla was struggling like a fish on a hook. And with just about as much effect, she pondered furiously, as he thrust her through the big car's still-open driver's door and in a rough voice bade her,

'Get over to the other side!'

He had climbed in beside her and, before she had her seatbelt fastened, was swinging the car round to its own side of the road, then speeding off fast, away from Strathallane.

Consumed with outrage at his unspeakable arrogance, Isla turned in her seat to glare at his profile with its dishevelled dark hair and glittering dark eyes. 'I already asked you this, so kindly answer me. Where the hell do you think you're taking me?'

He kept his eyes on the road and did not even deign to glance at her. 'I'm taking you somewhere where we can talk,' he answered gruffly. 'As I told you, you and I have unfinished business.'

Isla laughed without humour. 'That's where you're mistaken. The last piece of business I shall ever have with you is lying at this moment in your driveway. In tiny chewed-up pieces, I sincerely hope.'

At that he did turn round for an instant, sardonic amusement flickering in his eyes. 'That was something I thought I'd never witness—the editor supreme, Isla MacDonald, she for whom her work is the essence of her being, flinging a bag full of precious editorial files underneath the wheels of a car.' He raised one dark eyebrow. 'I was impressed.'

Hastily Isla jerked her eyes away from him, as the reason for that dramatic, quite spontaneous action—one that, on reflection, surprised her too— suddenly all came flooding back to her. The sight of Evelyn in the conservatory. The sight of Evelyn heavy with Rory's child.

A chilling nausea that started in her stomach seemed to rise up to the back of her throat. Impressed he may be, but he would never know the secret in her past that had driven her to it.

In a low voice she told him, 'I don't know what you're up to, but you're wasting your time with this little journey. Whatever it is you have to say to me, I can assure you I have no wish to hear it.'

'That's as maybe, but hear it you shall.' He glanced across at her, his expression grim. 'Every damned word of it, from start to finish.'

It looked as though she would have no choice but to hear him, for they had long ago left the main road now and were twisting and turning along narrow side-roads, their progress hushed by the carpet of snow. However much she might wish to escape him, she was virtually his prisoner.

She slanted him a look of total censure. 'I may have to hear, but I don't have to listen.'

'You'll do both.' His tone was gritty as he turned to look at her. 'You'll damned well stay locked inside this car until you've listened to and understood fully every single word I have to say to you.'

'Then we might be here for quite some time.' Isla's gaze locked defiantly with his. 'Since you seem to suffer from an almost pathological inability to say exactly what you mean, it's just conceivable I might have some difficulty in understanding you.'

He turned back to his driving with a weary sort of smile. 'Don't worry, I intend to make myself perfectly clear.'

They had left behind all signs of habitation. As they climbed ever higher up the hillside, Isla could see below them, scattered like tenpins, the farm houses and outbuildings of the Vale of Strathallane. Ahead of them was snowclad forest. Wild, empty moorland flanked them on both sides.

As Isla glanced around her, she felt a prickle of apprehension—not for the isolation of the spot where he had taken her, for she had absolutely no fear of being alone with Rory, but rather for what he was about to tell her. In spite of the impetuosity that characterised his nature, it was not his way to make unnecessary dramas. And the way he had kidnapped her and brought her here could be described in no other way than dramatic. Whatever it was he had to tell her, it clearly mattered to him a great deal that she should hear it.

He came at last to a silent halt on a sort of promontory, overlooking the vale, pulled on the hand-brake and unbuckled his seatbelt. Without preamble, he turned to look at her.

'I know why you ran away,' he said.

'Oh, really?' Her heart gave a little leap.

'You ran away because you saw Evelyn.'

She paused a heartbeat. 'Is that what you think?' Suddenly, she could not look at him.

'That's what I think. Tell me, is it true?'

As far as it went, it was true enough. It was the sight of Evelyn that had triggered her flight— though why the sight of a pregnant Evelyn should have had that effect on her was something that only she could know.

She shrugged dismissively. 'What does it matter? It was hardly worth your chasing after me like that. I left the files for you, after all. What more do you want?'

There was a pause. He sighed. 'There's something I have to tell you.' Then he reached out one hand and caught her jaw lightly and gently forced her head round to face him. 'Look at me, Isla,' he commanded softly, as she continued to keep her eyes averted. 'I want you to look at me and to listen to what I'm saying.'

With an effort she raised her eyes to his, feeling her heart clench within her as she met his tawny gaze. She had seen that look in his eyes before, that look of almost agonised intensity that presaged some heartfelt declaration. In the past she had seen it when he had told her he loved her, when he had vowed that one day they would be married. And seeing it now she felt a sharp stab of sorrow. Whatever it was he was about to tell her she would find very difficult to believe.

She blinked once and told him, 'I'm listening. Speak.'

He sat back a little and drew his hand away, letting his fingers brush softly against her cheek in a fleeting, momentary caress, and she could see that there was a tautness about his jaw and a slight frown marring his smooth, high forehead.

'I wanted to tell you this before,' he said. 'I tried, but the moment was never right.'

Isla's pulse was suddenly racing, ticking like a time bomb about to explode. She felt like closing her eyes, covering her ears and curling herself up into a tight, defensive ball. Didn't he realise there was nothing he could say to her that she could possibly want to hear? He was putting himself through this torture for nothing. And even more futilely he was inflicting it on her. It was an effort to keep looking at him as he continued,

'As I said at the beginning, I know what made you run. You saw Evelyn in the conservatory. It must have made you think of a lot of things.'

An involuntary blush stained Isla's cheek. She felt a flutter of panic. Did he know, after all? But she knew that he could not. She took a deep breath. 'It made me think that you're a rotten liar.'

'You say that because you saw she's pregnant?'

'Well guessed!' She allowed a sneer to tinge her voice. 'Married couples who live like strangers don't go around having babies together!'

A smile touched his lips. 'I can't deny that. But there's one small point I'd like to make——'

Isla cut through him. 'Why did you lie? I wasn't even interested in the state of your marriage!'

'If you'll just let me finish——'

'Why did you lie to me?'

'I didn't lie.'

'You did! You lied!'

'I didn't lie. It isn't my baby.'

Mid-protest Isla's jaw dropped open. 'What do you mean, it isn't your baby?'

'It isn't my baby.' He smiled again, wryly. 'And Evelyn is not my wife.'

A silence descended, as perfect and as total as the mid-winter silence that lay all around them. As Isla blinked back at him she felt numb to her toenails. She had been right about one thing. What he had just told her was unbelievable. And more than unbelievable, quite incomprehensible. Her brain was no more capable of absorbing his revelation than it was a tract in Cantonese.

He reached for her hand and held it lightly. 'I realise it must come as something of a surprise, but Evelyn and I have been divorced for several months.'

A surprise, he called it! It sounded like a fairy-tale. 'I don't believe you,' she responded uncertainly.

'I don't really blame you, but I can promise you it's true. The baby she's expecting is another man's.'

'But she's living in your house!' It was utterly ridiculous! 'People who are divorced don't live together!'

'We don't.' He sighed and shook his head. 'Since the divorce, we have neither spent a night under the same roof nor even so much as shared a dinner table. I come here from time to time to pick up clothes and things, but I sleep in the office—I have a makeshift bedroom there—or, occasionally, at my mother's house, as I did over Christmas.'

Isla stared at him dumbfounded. 'But why?' she demanded. 'Why would you choose to live like that?'

Rory took a deep breath. 'It's a crazy situation and perhaps I should never have let her talk me into it, but this man she's going to marry is already married, he's in the process of getting a divorce. To complicate matters, he's working in Saudi, and, because of the very strict laws they have there, there's no way Evelyn would be permitted to join him until she's legally his wife.

'She discovered she was pregnant just a month or so before our own divorce came through, and since no one in Strathallane knew about the divorce—I made sure it was all done most discreetly—she persuaded me to let her stay on at the house and let people go on believing we were still married.'

Isla shook her head. 'But why do such a thing? Why didn't she just go off and have her baby?'

'Quite frankly, there was nowhere for her to go. Her parents were both killed a couple of years ago, and, as you know, she has no brothers and sisters...' He shook his head. 'She's not strong like you, Isla. She told me she couldn't cope on her own, and, quite frankly, I believed her. Strathallane isn't the most liberal of places. People here frown on unmarried mothers. They might have given her a bit of a hard time.'

Isla was watching him, her heart in turmoil, struggling to come to terms with all these new revelations.

Rory was divorced. He had no marriage. He had no marriage and he had no wife. Through her confusion at all the complications regarding Evelyn, suddenly she felt giddy with relief. This man whose kisses she had so longed for was as free to love as she was herself.

She felt the sun break through a cloud in her heart. She wanted to sing and shout and dance.

But Rory was frowning at her. 'Do you understand, Isla? Do you understand why I did it? She really did have nowhere to go.'

Isla nodded. 'I understand.' She could remember now her mother telling her about the tragedy of

Evelyn's parents. But, all the same, she couldn't resist adding with just a hint of acid in her voice, 'It was convenient that she had such an obliging ex-husband who was prepared to put himself out for her.' She paused and threw him a narrow look. 'You must be very fond of her still.'

The hand that held hers grew tight around her fingers. Rory's dark eyes regarded her intently. 'I'm fond of her, but not in the way you mean. Our marriage was a sham from the very beginning. A more ill-matched couple would be hard to imagine—and, in fact, the two of us had been living like strangers long before she met this new man of hers.' He sighed. 'At least it meant the divorce was amicable. Both of us wanted out of the marriage. She was only too happy to let me sue for adultery, and I was only too happy to oblige.'

His fingers laced with hers as he let out a sigh. 'Perhaps I was stupid to let her talk me into this arrangement, but it was never meant to go on for so long. At the time when I agreed to let her stay on at the house I was just about to start a six-month stint in the States. Evelyn promised me she would be gone before I got back.' He pulled a face. 'Unfortunately, she wasn't—some hitch, apparently, with her boyfriend's divorce. What could I do? She was eight months pregnant. I could scarcely throw her out on the street.'

He sighed. 'However, she assures me now that it'll only be a matter of a few more weeks. I hope to hell she's right. I've had enough of the whole thing. Camping out in the office is no joke. I have to keep pretending to everyone that I'm working late.' He sighed again. 'All that is bad enough, but since you showed up it's been absolute hell.'

Suddenly, he was reaching for her, gathering her to him. 'I wanted you so badly and yet I couldn't tell you.' He kissed her forehead, her cheek, her nose, then he paused to kiss each eyelid in turn. 'Oh, Isla, I've missed you!' He held her close to him. 'It's so wonderful to be with you again!'

Isla sank against him with a sob in her throat as all the pain inside her melted away. And suddenly she knew why in eight long years there had been no other love in her life. Not, as she had believed, because she had been afraid to love or because she had lost the ability to trust. The truth, as it turned out, was a great deal simpler.

The man who right this minute held her in his arms was the only man she could ever love.

CHAPTER EIGHT

'WHAT an absolute beast you are! Why didn't you tell me right away?'

'Because you didn't want to know. At least I thought you didn't. And, anyway, as I told you, the whole things's supposed to be a secret.'

Isla knotted her fingers in Rory's dark hair and gave it a not-so-gentle tug. 'You could have told me on Hogmanay! I might even have allowed you to kiss me if you had!'

'Does that mean I can kiss you now?' Rory leaned towards her, his eyes darkening as he gazed at her.

All at once Isla's heart grew still. She had been waiting for this moment for eight long years. She could scarcely believe it had finally come. Dry-mouthed, she nodded. 'I wish you would. If you don't kiss me, I'm going to kiss you.'

Rory needed no second invitation. Gently, firmly, he drew her towards him, pausing for a second to let his eyes burn into hers. 'Happy New Year,' he murmured throatily. Then her soul lit up with every colour of the rainbow as his mouth at last came down on hers.

Happiness flooded her. She was so glad she had waited. For now that all his secrets were out, now that she knew he was not married, the magic of his kiss was infinitely sweeter than it could ever have been before.

And she had forgotten how sweet a kiss could be. How sweet, how thrilling, how powerful, how wild. She had forgotten how one's limbs felt when they turned to powder and that aching throb of almost unbearable excitement when the blood in one's veins turned to liquid fire.

But in an instant, as his strong arms pressed her to him, making her heartbeat turn to thunder in her breast, all those long-forgotten ecstasies came cascading back to her. She clung to him as though she would never let him go.

His lips feathered hers, hungry and persuasive, making her shudder for the wanting of him and gasp deep in her throat. Then his mouth grew harder, urgent and greedy, his tongue flicking lightly against her teeth until she sighed in surrender and allowed him entry.

That sudden raw contact sent sparks shooting through her, burning her senses, igniting her loins. Then she cried out with helpless pleasure as his hand slid beneath the folds of her coat to take possession of one eager, swollen breast.

Through the thin silk of her blouse Isla felt a sensation like fifteen million volts of electricity charging through her. She shivered in ecstasy, pressing against him, as with the heel of his hand he circled slowly while his fingers sought the stiff, hard peak. And the longing in her was suddenly quite unbearable. Her whole body was screaming for the final act of love.

For she knew that this ecstasy she was experiencing was nothing compared to what Rory could offer. And she longed now for them to cast their garments from them and lie together naked in each other's arms. To feel his flesh against her flesh, to taste him, to touch him, and finally to abandon herself, willingly and totally, to that ultimate, incomparable joining together that she had experienced with no other man since him.

He seemed to read her mind. He pushed back her hair, his eyes glowing with passion as he looked into her face. 'I've never made love in a car before...but I'm willing, if you are, my love.'

'Oh, yes,' she murmured. 'I want you, Rory.'

He kissed her fiercely. 'Then you shall have me. I'm yours.'

It seemed a long time later that they lay together, half dressed now, on the front seat of the car. From the CD player a Mozart symphony was playing and outside the snow was falling gently, like a fragile curtain, cutting the world off. A glow of perfect happiness surrounded them. No two people in the entire universe were more at peace.

Rory ran one finger down the side of her jaw, then let it trail down her neck, making her shiver. He drew her a little closer to him.

'There's something else I have to tell you,' he said.

Isla looked up into the smoky depths of the dark tawny eyes that held her mesmerised. His touch was like fire against her skin. 'In that case, you'd better tell me,' she sighed.

'It's about that field. Jock Campbell's field. That building you were so keen to force me into dropping the plans for... I have a confession to make. There were never any plans.'

'No plans?' Isla blinked uncomprehendingly back at him. 'What do you mean there were no plans?'

'Just that.' He smiled and kissed her brow, his hands idly, wickedly, caressing her breasts. 'It was never my intention to build on that land. That was why I couldn't promise to drop my plans.' He dropped kisses on her nose, her chin, her breastbone, then paused to catch one aching peak between his teeth. 'As I said, there were never any plans to drop.'

Isla felt the breath catch in her throat. A judder of exquisite pleasure went tearing through her. But she pulled herself back to the brink of sanity and demanded in a croaky voice, 'You mean you never intended to build all along? Then why on earth did you buy the land?'

The tawny eyes twinkled as he raised his head to look at her. He nuzzled a kiss in the crevice of her neck. 'I bought it precisely in order to ensure that it would never be built on by anyone else. As you yourself so eloquently argued, such an eventuality would be a total desecration.'

It took a millisecond for the enormity of what he was saying to sink in. Isla drew herself up a little to examine him more closely. 'Is what you're telling me really the truth?'

'Of course it's the truth. Why would I lie?'

'But why should you care what happens to that land? Why should you go to all that trouble? And why didn't you tell me right at the start?'

Rory smiled and slid one arm around her shoulders. With his free hand he caressed her cheek. 'That's quite a formidable battery of questions. Which one would you like me to answer first?'

Isla scowled at him, mock angry. 'Why didn't you tell me right at the start?'

'Because you were being so bossy, so damned high and mighty. When you came stomping into my office that day, making demands left, right and centre, I decided to take you down a peg or two.' He caught her jaw with his fingers and looked long into her eyes, then bent to kiss each fluttering eyelid in turn. 'You know you have the most beautiful eyes? I'd forgotten just how beautiful. They're the colour of wild heather in full bloom.'

Then, as she sighed, remembering that that was how he had described them all those many years ago, he added in a voice that was soft and low, 'Later I devised that business of the magazine dummy just so I could have a legitimate excuse to keep seeing you. To tell the truth, I'd more or less decided to scrap it. I probably would have if you hadn't come along.'

He took her hand and raised it to his lips and kissed the fingers one by one. 'I had to see you and I knew you would never agree to it as long as you believed I was married, so I cooked up a way of making sure I could. Devious of me, I know.' He smiled unashamedly. 'But I can't say I'm sorry that I did.'

Oddly, Isla wasn't sorry either. She looked into his face with its clear, high brow, no longer marred by the tension of before, and let her eyes travel down the planes of his cheekbones, the faintly crooked nose, the firm, square jawline, and it was like a journey of rediscovery. No longer was she seeing what he had once been through the eyes of the young girl she no longer was. She was seeing him as he was now and she liked what she saw. She liked it immensely.

She allowed her eyes to flicker lower to his half-buttoned-up shirt and stretched out one finger to trace the broad pectorals with their scattering of dark hairs. 'I still believe you could have told me earlier that you weren't actually married any more. After all, you've told me now. So, what's the difference?' she enquired.

'The difference is that at the start I didn't really see any point in telling you. Whether I was married or not didn't appear to have any relevance. You made it very clear that you didn't want to know me in any circumstances. The fact that you believed I was married wasn't an issue. But then later...' He smiled and caught her hand and kissed the inside of her wrist. 'But then,' he continued, 'I sensed a softening in your attitude. Just the tiniest hint of a chink in your chainmail...'

As he paused to look down at her with those golden eagle eyes, so proud, so splendid, just like the man himself, Isla knew in her heart that he had judged her correctly. Yet it was hard to remember the reason for her antagonism and equally hard to recall what had caused her to change. But for the moment, this blessed moment, here at peace in his arms, she had no desire to tax her brain with such questions. Instead, she listened with rapt attention as he continued, 'So I tried to tell you, but you wouldn't let me. You went rushing off like an out-raged snowcat, no doubt ruining a good pair of shoes in the process, screaming at me to leave you alone.'

He was referring to that little episode at Glenshee. And he was right about one thing, her sandals had been ruined. She poked him in the ribs and made a face at him. 'You could have come after me, if you'd really been keen!'

'And risk another scene like that scene in the high street? No, thank you.' He shook his head and kissed her. 'I decided to wait for a more propitious moment.' His expression suddenly sobered. 'But I very nearly blew it. If this afternoon I hadn't gone to pick up some things at the house and discovered you having a tantrum in the driveway, I might never have had another chance. I've a feeling the thaw might have gone sharply into reverse.'

Isla smiled. 'I've a feeling you're right.' She didn't bother to enlighten him that the reason for her visit was that the thaw, as he called it, had already gone into reverse, and she had been planning to disappear forever. Instead, she asked him, 'What about those files and things? I hope you didn't leave them lying in the driveway?'

'I'm afraid I did. I came straight after you. Quite frankly, I didn't give a damn about the files.'

'After all that hard work I put into them! How very remiss of you to leave them lying in the snow!' But as he pulled her to him, the fate of the files was the very last thing that concerned her. Suddenly in her head she was quickly undoing the plans for her departure that she had made. She would not, after all, be leaving tomorrow. In fact, the way she was feeling now, she would not be leaving at all unless Rory asked her to leave!

He was cradling her in his arms, looking down at her, as though nothing could be further from his mind. Smiling, he smoothed the hair back from her brow and looked long and deep into her face. 'You didn't seriously believe that I would allow anyone to build in that field next to your parents, let alone, surely, that I would do so myself? I have an enormous affection for your parents. We were very close once, if you remember.'

Oh, Isla remembered. No doubt about that. In the old days Rory had been a constant visitor to the cottage, at one point almost like one of the family. And the affection he'd spoken of had been mutual. Her mother, especially, had adored him.

Isla told him now, 'I thought perhaps *you* had forgotten. It has been a long time, after all.'

'There are some things one never forgets,' he assured her. He let his fingers trace the curve of her bosom, then cupped one firm, full orb with his palm. 'Among them how wonderful it feels to make love to you. And the reality, I promise you, more than lives up to the memory. Making love with you is the most beautiful thing.'

'Making love with you is beautiful, too.'

She smiled and slid her hands beneath the loose cotton shirt, letting her fingers explore the warm, hard flesh. He had the most beautiful body it was possible to imagine, tight and muscular, vibrant and strong, and she could feel it respond now to her touch, as a shiver went through him from head to foot.

His arms about her tightened. His hands were in her hair. 'Now that we've discovered how to make love in a car, what do you say we do it again?'

Isla looked into his eyes as the love flooded through her, that wonderful love that had never died.

'Oh, yes,' she murmured. 'Darling Rory.' Then she closed her eyes. 'Love me,' she sighed.

It was as though those eight years had never been. As though all the warmth and the closeness between them had simply been suspended for a while, waiting in some recess of their hearts to be brought back to life when the right time came.

After they had made love again, rediscovering one another, touching, caressing, worshipping, kissing, they lay together in one another's arms, oblivious of the snow that still fell all around them, safe in the privacy of the big warm car, sharing confidences and quietly reminiscing.

'Remember that time we drove to Glen Clova for a picnic in that flashy red MG Midget of yours...?'

Rory laughed. 'We put the hood down and then we couldn't get it up again...'

'And then, of course, it started to rain! Do you remember that absolute deluge? I arrived home looking like a drowned rat. I'm sure my mother thought we'd been swimming!'

'In the middle of April? She must have thought we were crazy!'

'She did,' Isla laughed. 'And I suppose we were a little. We were always doing crazy things.'

Rory squeezed her and kissed her. 'Speak for yourself.' Then he added mock seriously, 'You know, it took me the best part of a fortnight to get the upholstery properly dried out.'

'And it took me the best part of a fortnight to recover from the cold I caught!'

'And you loved every minute of it,' Rory teased her. 'I don't seem to remember hearing any complaints about the daily supplies of chocolates and flowers I brought you!'

As she looked into his eyes, Isla's heart contracted. It had been so long ago and yet the memory was so vivid—and it was just one sweet memory among millions. He had always been so good to her, so generous, so thoughtful. It had been part of the magic and the charm of him that no other man had come even close to matching.

She reached out and touched his cheek with her fingertips, gasping with pleasure as he caught her fingers and kissed them. And what had come to her in a flash of inspiration just a short time ago when he had first kissed her seemed to settle within her like an absolute truth. The reason she had never managed to fall in love again was because she had never really fallen out of love with Rory.

So much for the hate she had believed she bore him! That had been nothing but a self-protective disguise!

She had believed that he had blighted her heart and made her incapable of loving. But it had not been loving of which she had been incapable, simply of loving anyone else.

The knowledge warmed that cold corner of her soul that had so agonised over all those barren romances. She knew now why, time after time, she had become involved with the wrong sort of man. Not simply because she had been afraid to love again, though that, undoubtedly, had been a part of it. Subtly, subconsciously, her heart had been telling her that to search for love elsewhere would be a pointless exercise.

For her heart bore the indelible stamp of one man. Like it or not, it was already spoken for.

Yet, intermingled with the relief Isla felt to discover that her string of romantic fiascos had a perfectly logical explanation, was a faint but very real thread of hurt and resentment. While she had eschewed all sexual involvement, leading an exemplary single existence, the man for whom her heart had secretly pined most assuredly had not done likewise.

While she had languished, chaste and solitary, he, without a thought, had taken a wife. A wife, presumably, whom he had once loved and, for at least part of the six years, had shared a bed with. Suddenly, a cloud seemed to darken her happiness. All at once she felt jealous of Evelyn.

She frowned at him now and in a small voice ventured, 'I've always wondered. Why did you marry Evelyn?'

Rory sighed and leaned back a little. 'I suppose the real answer is stupidity. I had no idea what I was walking into. I thought that I could make it work.'

'But surely you loved her?' The question pained her, but it was a question, nevertheless, that she had to ask.

'Perhaps a little, in the beginning. But if I did it didn't last.' He smiled at her lop-sidedly, touching her hair with his hand, letting his fingers trace the soft curve of her hairline. 'I started going out with Evelyn a few months after you left for London—

or, to be more precise, soon after that time I came to see you at your flat in Ladbroke Grove.' He shook his head and frowned a little, conjuring up between them, without the need for words, the memory of that unhappy meeting.

Isla glanced away, loath to recall all the hurt and desolation she had felt that day. He had dropped in to see her while passing through London just to ask if she was OK. And she had been far from OK. She had been close to rock-bottom, still raw and bleeding deep within her from the tragedy of her recent loss.

But she had told him nothing, not wishing to burden him when he had made it so clear that he wished to be free of her. And that had been when she had begun the process of distilling her love for him into hate. Only the process had failed, she realised now. Her love had proved more durable than she might have wished.

Determinedly, she blinked away the ghosts. What had happened that day was best forgotten. And yet, illogically, as she looked into his eyes, she had an almost uncontrollable desire finally to confide in him. Then the secret she had carried with her for so long would at last be *their* secret, as it should have been all along.

But still she hesitated, just a little afraid. I'll tell him when the time is right, she promised herself. Very soon, but not just yet.

He was leaning to kiss her on the brow, his lips warm and tingle-making as he continued, 'It was Evelyn who, from the start, pushed for marriage, and I stupidly allowed myself to be talked into it. There was also quite a lot of pressure from our families. Everyone seemed to think we were the perfect match.'

As he pulled a face, Isla reflected wryly what a relief that must have been to him after all the hassle of his mother's opposition to her. But somehow she found it no consolation to learn that he'd been influenced by Elizabeth's wishes. All it did was reinforce the uncomfortable suspicion that his mother's frank dislike of her had been partly responsible for the break-up of their relationship.

That thought sat uneasily within her. She had never really wanted to believe it. For, whatever other faults he had, she had always believed Rory to be entirely his own man.

'Anyway, we had a couple of almost tolerable years,' he continued on the saga of his marriage, 'but then everything started to go downhill fast. Three years ago we started sleeping in separate bedrooms, and that was the beginning of the end. Eighteen months ago Evelyn met this guy she's going to marry, and for both of us it wasn't a moment too soon. It forced us to start talking seriously about divorce, something we really should have done years ago.'

He shrugged and sighed. 'But enough of that. What we ought to be discussing right now is you and me and how we plan to spend the rest of the evening.' He grinned and held up his wrist to show her the time on his watch, then laughed as she blinked and gasped in surprise.

'I'd no idea it was so late! Good grief, it's almost seven o'clock!' She had been vaguely aware that it had been dark for some time, but it grew dark very early at this time of year.

'You see how time flies when you're enjoying yourself?' He straightened and drew Isla up alongside him, smoothing her tangled hair with one delicate hand. 'You'd better tidy yourself up, young lady,' he instructed jokingly, 'if you want me to take you out to dinner.'

'Dinner? What a good idea! But what about my reputation?' she enquired teasingly, poking him in the ribs, as she did up her blouse. 'The world still believes you're a married man!'

'We'll go somewhere quiet. I know just the place. All candle-light and soft music. How does that appeal?'

'It appeals magnificently,' Isla assured him, pulling down the sun visor to glance at her reflection in the mirror and feeling a stab of strange poignancy go darting through her at the unfamiliar vision that met her gaze.

It was years since she had seen her eyes with such a sparkle, or such a warm flush of colour in her cheeks. And that in spite of virtually no make-up, for pretty well all of it had been kissed off! Yet her whole being glowed with a heady kind of radiance, as though she might ignite whatever she touched.

She delved into her bag and pulled out her hair-brush, then pulled it through her shiny chestnut hair. She gave her head a shake and held the brush out to Rory. 'Help yourself,' she offered, smiling. 'I'm not the only one around here who needs tidying up.'

He took the brush and caught her outstretched hand simultaneously and drew her with a gentle tug towards him. 'Isla, Isla, if only you knew how much I've missed you.'

He crushed her against him, his lips seeking hers, the fingers of his free hand sweeping through her hair. At his touch her scalp tingled with delicious sensations. 'I've missed you, too,' she murmured huskily.

It was fully half an hour later before they were ready to leave. Rory handed back her brush. 'How do I look? Will I do?' he enquired, smiling.

Isla threw him a quick look, her heart skipping inside her. It was difficult to say which version of him she found more attractive—the decidedly dishevelled figure of a moment or two ago, dark hair tousled, shirt undone, his tie hanging loosely about his neck and a fair expanse of muscular bronzed chest on display, or the smooth-haired Rory who sat beside her now, shirt and tie once more in order, a devilish twinkle in his golden eagle eyes. Either version was immeasurably to her taste in a way that made the hairs on the back of her neck stand on end.

She took the brush from him and returned it to her bag. 'You'll do,' she assured him, averting her eyes.

Rory took the road slowly, manoeuvring the big car with easy expertise over the snow. He glanced across at her. 'Do you want to stop off at the cottage and let your parents know what's happening? We'll have to take the car back anyway.'

Good heavens! Her parents' Renault! She'd forgotten all about it! 'It'll be buried up to its hub-caps by now!' she suggested worriedly. Then she answered his question. 'Yes, I suppose I'd better.'

Though mantled in freshly fallen snow, the Renault in fact was none the worse for its brief abandonment. Isla breathed a sigh of relief as it started first time and she set off along the road behind the Jaguar.

It was an unwelcome feeling being alone again, she pondered, as she followed the red tail-lights across the snow. A cold, uncertain, unnatural feeling. Being with Rory again had felt so right.

But she must tell him her secret, she reminded herself sharply. After all, in a way, he had a right to know. And, besides, she had borne it alone for too long now. To share it would be a blessed relief.

Over dinner, she decided. That was when she would do it. The moment she felt the time was right.

At the cottage Isla parked the Renault in the drive and shook her head as Rory slid down his window and enquired, 'Do you want me to come in with you, just to say hello?'

'Not just now. Some other time. Otherwise we'll never make it to dinner.' There would be time enough for her parents to learn about this miraculous reconciliation. Right now it would require too many explanations.

It only took her five minutes to pop into the cottage and explain somewhat cryptically that she was going out for dinner, adding as she headed once more for the door, 'Oh, by the way, Jock Campbell's field . . . I'll explain it all in detail to you later, but your worries are over. There's to be no building.'

Then she was hurrying back outside again and climbing into the Jaguar, feeling its warmth close around her like a cocoon and her heart burst with foolish happiness inside her as Rory leaned to kiss her and murmured, 'Welcome back. What took you so long?' He grinned as he twined his fingers lovingly with hers and raised them softly to his lips. 'You mustn't keep leaving me alone like that.'

They drove to a small country hotel about twenty miles outside Strathallane, all flickering candle-light and soft music, just as Rory had promised her. They were shown to a table in a quiet corner and, as the waiter handed them their menus, Rory leaned across the table and told her, 'This is the first time I've ever been here. I've been saving it up for some special occasion.' He winked across at her. 'From now on it'll be strictly Isla's and Rory's.'

Isla's and Rory's. Isla smiled back at him, feeling a warm, tingly feeling spread within her. Isla's and Rory's was the seal of approval they'd once put on all their special places. Picnic spots among the heather, hilltop hideaways where they would lie together, the occasional restaurant that took their fancy.

They were places reserved strictly for the two of them together, places where they never took their friends or families. And it was years since Isla had heard the expression, though she'd remembered it, wistfully, on occasion.

Isla's and Rory's.

To hear Rory use it now filled her with happiness and a kind of heady, reckless optimism. It spoke of sharing and togetherness and a very special kind of relationship. It seemed to hint at some kind of future.

But before leaping into the future she must deal with the past. She still had to tell him about her secret.

But first, let them enjoy their meal together. She would tell him over the coffee, when they were both feeling mellow, when this new rapport between them had strengthened even further. For it was important that her revelation should not spoil things between them. Perhaps, if handled correctly, it might even draw them closer together.

The meal was utterly delicious, though neither of them paid much heed to what they were eating, each was so totally engrossed in the other. It was just like the old days, Isla thought happily, as the waiter cleared away their dessert plates and brought them coffee. And possibly that was why she continued to procrastinate. The thought of what she must tell him made her just a little bit nervous.

The coffee-cups in turn were taken away and a brandy brought for Rory, with a Glayva Highland liqueur for Isla. And Isla was aware of a mounting tension within her as Rory proceeded to launch into an enthusiastic account of his true plans for Jock Campbell's field. Time was running out. She would have to speak soon. But she listened with a smile as he proceeded to tell her, 'My plan all along was to rent it out to the local pony club. They're short of space, so I understand, and they're looking for somewhere where their older members can practise jumping and that sort of thing. The field is only half a mile from the stables. I think it would be ideal for them.'

Isla nodded. 'I think so, too.' But her mind was only barely focused on what he was saying. She had been putting off and waiting for an opening for long enough. It was time to take the bull by the horns.

He was smiling across at her, oblivious of her dilemma. 'I hope your parents won't object to having the pony club for neighbours?'

'I'm sure they won't. Not in the least. On the contrary, I suspect they'll rather like it.'

He winked across at her. 'That's what I thought. I remember your father used to be a bit of a rider himself.'

As he smiled into her eyes, she felt the love wash through. She had misjudged him so badly over the business of the field. Perhaps she had misjudged him over many other things. She had withheld her secret from him, fearing he might prefer not to know, but perhaps she had been wrong about that as well. And perhaps her current nervousness was all for nothing.

As he opened his mouth to speak, Isla leaned across the table and touched his arm softly. 'Rory...' she began.

At her earnest expression Rory frowned and laid his hand on top of hers. 'What is it, Isla?' he enquired.

Isla swallowed, her heart beating like a drum. For better or for worse the moment had finally come for her to unburden herself of the pain and the shame that she had carried around with her for eight long years. She had wondered at least a million times how that would feel. Now she was about to find out.

She cleared her throat and stared down at the tablecloth, gathering her courage for a moment. Then, dry-mouthed, she looked up into the deep tawny eyes that were regarding her with a rapt expression, and in a voice that seemed to come from far away, almost as though it belonged to someone else, she said, 'Rory, I have something to tell you.'

CHAPTER NINE

'WHAT is it, Isla?' Rory's tone was concerned as he leaned across the table towards her. 'What is it that you have to tell me?'

As Isla looked into his face she knew that she had been waiting for this moment for eight long years. Yet, now that it had come, her nerve was threatening to desert her. All at once her palms were damp and clammy. She felt as though she could not speak.

What if he refused to believe her, called her a liar, accused her of invention? What if he laughed at her? What if he mocked? What if he told her he couldn't care less?

For a moment she was tempted to cover her tracks and come out with some inconsequential confession. Anything to avoid the pain and the humiliation that any one of these reactions would bring down on her head.

But she had to tell him. It was his right to know. Shakily, she let out her breath and smiled apologetically across at him. 'What I have to tell you ... It's not easy.'

He squeezed her hand kindly. 'I can see that. And don't feel you have to if you'd rather not.' The golden eagle eyes looked into hers and he seemed to be offering her his strength and his reassurance. 'But if you do want to tell me, I'm listening,' he said softly. 'Just take your time. We've got all night.'

Isla licked her lips and her voice was unsteady as she forced herself to go on to tell him, 'It's something that happened a long time ago. Eight years ago, to be precise.'

'I see.' He raised one jet-black eyebrow and continued to watch her with quiet composure. 'Eight years ago is indeed a long time—but a time that, like you, I have not forgotten.'

At the sympathy and encouragement in his tone, Isla felt her courage returning. But still she hedged. 'I would have told you at the time, but things were a little difficult between us...'

As she paused, he nodded. 'Yes, they were.' He looked deep into her eyes. 'So, what was it, Isla?'

A pulse was beating in her throat, as though at any moment it might explode. She stared dumbly at her hand that he still held against his arm, wondering if she should draw it away. She kept staring and wondering as she told him tonelessly, 'Shortly before I left Strathallane to go down to London, I made a certain discovery...'

'Discovery? What discovery?' He was watching her closely and she could feel the pulse in her neck beat faster.

'I made the discovery...' Again she paused.

He waited in silence.

'That I was pregnant.'

For a moment it was as though the earth had gone still. A silence fell between them, so profound and so shocking it seemed to swallow every breath of air between them. Isla looked into his face and felt a chill spread through her at the raw expression in his eyes. It was an expression that was somehow both stunned and vivid. She had never seen anything like it before.

When he spoke at last his voice was ragged. 'You're telling me that you were...pregnant?'

Stiffly, Isla nodded.

'And you didn't tell me?'

It was not a question. It was an accusation. Instantly Isla defended herself with an accusation of her own. 'I didn't tell you because you wouldn't have been interested. During that period you weren't much interested in anything to do with our relationship. All you cared about was Buchanan's.'

He ignored her allegation and his dark frown deepened as he leaned across the table and demanded, 'And what about the baby? What happened to it?'

Isla felt her stomach tighten. She dropped her eyes. 'I lost it,' she answered.

'*Lost* it?' He ground the question out at her and there was a world of condemnation in his tone. 'Are you trying to tell me that's why you went to London? In order to rid yourself of our child?'

At the crude accusation Isla's eyes shot up. 'I'm trying to tell you nothing of the kind!' How dared he make such a foul suggestion when she had wanted that baby with all her heart? Her voice was shaky as she continued, 'Getting rid of the baby, as you so crudely put it, was something that never even crossed my mind. I intended having it. But I lost it.' Her voice broke as a wave of pain washed through her as vivid and real as eight years ago. She had to fight back the tears that pricked at her eyes, as she ended jaggedly, 'I had a miscarriage.'

For a long shimmering moment their eyes locked together and he seemed to be searching deep into her soul. Her mouth dry with emotion, Isla frowned at him. 'Surely you don't believe I had an abortion? Surely you couldn't believe that of me?'

The tawny eyes narrowed for a fraction of a second, then Rory sighed and leaned back in his chair. 'No, I don't believe that. I'm sorry I suggested it.' Then he sighed again and ran a hand across his hair. His tone was acid with irony as he told her, 'Forgive me, but this whole thing's just a bit of a shock. How could you have kept it from me all these years?'

Isla's heart was thumping. 'I told you why. You wouldn't have wanted to know.'

Rory watched her in silence for a moment, the tawny eyes dissecting beneath the black wings of his brows. 'Like hell I wouldn't. The child was mine. I think I had a right to know.'

She'd thought so too. That was why she'd told him now. But then it had all been very different. Isla looked back at him steadily, resenting his tone. 'It's a little late now to start talking about your rights. Neither your rights nor your responsibilities appeared to concern you much then.'

'I wasn't given the chance.' His tone was steely.

'You wouldn't have wanted it,' she insisted. Her tone was steely too. 'As I said before, Buchanan's was all you cared about. You didn't want to know about anything else.'

The dark jaw tightened just a fraction. He pushed aside his half-empty brandy glass as though he longed to hurl it across the table. 'You're right, that's the second time you've said that! So what the hell is it supposed to mean?'

Such bare-faced innocence! Such bare-faced deceit! How dared he pretend he didn't know what she meant? In angry, staccato syllables she spelled it out to him.

'I mean that from the minute you inherited Buchanan's, your new exalted position was all that mattered to you. From the moment you took your seat in the precious boardroom I literally ceased to exist for you. One minute I was supposedly the most important thing in your life and the next I mattered less to you than the dust on your shoes!'

Through her anger her voice wavered as again she tasted all the old hurts and humiliations. 'To tell you the truth, I'm surprised you even noticed when I finally went off to London!'

'I'm surprised, too. You'd become more or less invisible over the last few weeks before you went.'

'Because you didn't want me! I can take a hint!'

'And whoever said I didn't want you?' Suddenly he was leaning across the table towards her, an intense look burning in his eyes. 'I don't deny that suddenly I had a lot of other things on my mind. The deaths of my father and Niall, following so close on one another, turned my whole world upside-down. Maybe I didn't give you all the attention I'd given you before, but that didn't mean I didn't want you any more.

'On the contrary...' He leaned back suddenly and regarded her through half-shuttered lids. 'There were times when I needed you unbearably, times when I was desperate for someone to talk to, but you were never there——' He broke off suddenly, almost impatiently, as though sensing that he was wasting his time with this explanation, and all softness had gone from his tone as he continued, 'And when you *were* there the only thing you were interested in talking about was this damned job you were applying for down in London! At the least opportunity you brought up the subject.'

Irritably, he tossed his napkin on the table. 'So, if I may just correct the record, *you* were the one who was busy dropping hints. *I* was the one who was being forced to pick up on them!'

Isla threw him a scathing smile. 'What a clever manipulator you are! You can almost make a total lie sound plausible. Too bad I can remember what actually happened!'

But her words were as ineffectual as his had been, for their conversation was fast disintegrating into a dialogue of the deaf, with neither paying heed to what the other was saying. Totally ignoring her rebuttal, Rory continued, 'And to think all that time you were pregnant with our baby and you didn't even have the decency to tell me.'

Isla glared across at him. 'I was doing you a favour. As you just said yourself, you had enough on your plate.'

'Of course I know why. It's suddenly quite clear to me. You didn't tell me about the baby because you knew I would stop you leaving Strathallane as long as you were carrying our child.' His tone was crushed gravel as he continued, the look in his eyes harsh and full of disdain. 'And that, of course, was something you weren't prepared to risk. You had your heart set on going to London and making a big name for yourself. Our child and its future would come a very poor second. I imagine it was quite a relief to you when you lost it.'

That was the cruellest thing he could have said. Her heart had broken that day she had miscarried and the wound had never properly healed. With a mammoth effort she fought back the tears that threatened now to spill from her eyes. One single tear would unleash a flood that she would never be able to control and she would die now before she would break down in front of him.

So she forced herself to answer him harshly, taking solace from the way he blanched a little at the shocking brutality of her words. 'Yes, it was something of a relief,' she answered levelly, wondering at the composure of her lie. 'The last thing I wanted was a lifelong reminder of you. After I left Strathallane I just wanted to forget you.'

'Yes, you made that very clear that time I came down to visit you in London! If I'd known the reception I was going to get, I think I would have saved myself the trouble!'

None of this was going as Isla had envisaged. The whole thing was disintegrating before her eyes and she could feel a bitter sense of sorrow rise up inside her as all she thought she had won back slipped inexorably away. She had imagined that her revelation would complete the circle of closeness between them, but instead it had opened the rift between them, wider even than before.

She had expected to feel unburdened by her confession, the heavy weight of her secret finally shed. But, perversely, she felt as though her burden had been doubled. Fresh pain and anger and resentment were suddenly tearing her apart.

And now he had dared to throw in her face that farcical meeting they'd had in London. And all the hurt and bewilderment of that day was bubbling up inside her, uncontrollably.

'What did you expect me to do? Throw my arms around you? Welcome you like some long-lost lover? Good lord!' She was outraged. 'You barely stayed for five minutes! Did you actually expect me to be over the moon because you so generously allowed me a few minutes of your time while you were passing through London on business?'

She gave a harsh laugh, remembering all the bitterness she'd felt when she'd opened up the door to him that day. It had been two weeks to the day since she'd been discharged from hospital after losing the baby, just over two months since she'd fled from Strathallane. She'd been feeling desperate with grief and shock and pain, afraid for the future, angry about the past and in no mood to respond to his familiar charming smile as he stood on her doorstep clutching a huge bunch of flowers.

She told him now, caustically, 'I'm so sorry if I disappointed you. But that was one little courtesy visit you would definitely have done better to have saved yourself!'

Rory regarded her through steely dark eyes. 'I think your memory is a little defective. I didn't stay for five minutes, I stayed for an hour, and I would have stayed longer if you hadn't made it so obvious that I wasn't welcome.'

'Would you indeed?' Isla met the dark gaze with uncompromising antipathy, as she was thrown back in her memory to relive the emotions of that day, the old wound inside her suddenly reopened, as fresh and as raw as it had been then. 'Tut, tut,' she mimicked cruelly. 'That would never have done. You might have missed one of your precious business appointments.'

Rory held her eyes. 'I had no appointments to miss. I wasn't down on business. I'd come to see you.'

Now whose memory was defective? Isla laughed without humour. 'It's pointless lying. I distinctly remember you saying that you were down on business and that you'd just happened to be passing and that was why you'd dropped in.'

Rory shook his head. 'Don't tell me you believed that? How the hell could I have just been passing through the middle of Ladbroke Grove when that's nowhere near the business centre of London?'

He was trying to confuse her and, in the process, endeavouring to rewrite history to suit himself. But Isla did not intend to allow him to get away with it. 'Then why did you say it?' she demanded hotly. 'Why didn't you just tell me you'd come to see me if, as you say, that was the truth?'

'Pride, I expect. You were so damned hostile. You made me feel as though every second of my company was an ordeal.'

'It was.' Isla glared at him, not believing one word. For some reason he was out to blame her for that particular débâcle, just as he seemed determined to blame her for everything else. But his attempt at a cover-up was a waste of time. The truth couldn't be altered just to suit his conscience.

Rory met her gaze without flinching. 'You could have told me about the baby then. Why the hell didn't you?' he demanded.

'There was no longer any baby to tell you about,' Isla answered, feeling the words catch in her throat. She steadied herself quickly and added crudely, 'Besides, perhaps I didn't feel it was any of your damned business.'

'None of my damned business?'

'That's what I said.'

'You were carrying a child of mine and you dare to say it was none of my damned business?' As he repeated the question and continued to stare at her, he seemed to be offering her the chance to reconsider her answer. An aura of menace shimmered about him. His patience, she could tell, was on a very short leash.

Isla stared back defiantly. 'Not only do I dare, I positively insist that it was none of your damned business. I'm just sorry I was stupid enough to tell you at all, for I still consider it to be none of your damned business. A man with your selfish, restricted outlook on life doesn't deserve to know such things!'

'You little bitch! You don't know what the hell you're talking about!' Suddenly he had reached across the table and grabbed her by the arm. His fingers dug into her flesh like pincers. The anger in his eyes drove through her like a laser. 'You're the one whose outlook on life is restricted! You've never given a thought to anyone but yourself!'

He held her eyes for a long, angry moment, then abruptly released her arm, almost thrusting her away. 'Let's get out of this place before I make a spectacle of myself.' With a snap of his fingers he summoned the waiter. 'The bill, please. In a hurry,' he commanded. And, without waiting, he began to push back his chair. 'We can continue this discussion somewhere more private,' he informed Isla. 'I'd rather not provide our fellow diners with a cabaret.'

On that last point Isla could not have agreed more. Already she had been increasingly aware that their discreetly raised voices were attracting attention. A public restaurant was no place for such a private confrontation. She followed him to the door with a sense of relief. But as soon as they were outside she was quick to inform him,

'I'd be grateful if you would just take me home now. I have no desire to pursue this discussion further. I think we've both said everything there is to be said.'

He waited until she was buckled into the front seat of the Jaguar before deigning to reply to her request. 'You may have said everything you have to say, but I've scarcely even begun yet,' he informed her, drawing away abruptly from the side of the road. 'Don't think you can wriggle out of this as easily as that.'

'There's nothing to wriggle out of.' Isla eyed him with hostility. 'And you're simply wasting your time by insisting on pursuing the subject. I have nothing more to say.'

'Wrong again.' He tossed her a hard look as they sped across the silent snow. 'Before this evening is through I intend finally to discover what the hell's going on inside that head of yours!'

Isla glanced away and stared out at the landscape, an unbroken, shimmering blanket of white, stretching as far as the eye could see. If only she knew herself what was inside her head. If only she could make any sense at all of her suddenly twisted and tangled emotions.

Just an hour ago, before all this had erupted, she had been feeling as happy as a fishmonger's cat. There had been love in her heart and hope for the future and a sense that at last she could put aside the past. The only reason she'd brought up the subject of the lost baby was so that she could purge it from her soul forever.

But she had made a fatal error. Far from purging the past, she had simply reawakened it, like some sleeping dinosaur that now in a fury of recriminations was trampling destructively all over the present.

The fault was Rory's. He had reacted unfairly, taking her by surprise with his anger and his accusations, turning on its head her attempt at appeasement, making her regret her rash decision to confide in him.

For his anger in turn had unleashed all her old resentments that, earlier today when he had held her in his arms, she had believed to be dead and buried forever. Like spectres leaping out at her from dark corners, they had set her emotions screaming within her so that she scarcely knew what to think any more. Just an hour ago she had known she loved him, that she had always loved him, that she could love no one else.

And she had thought that he might still love her, too. She had sensed it in his kisses and seemed to read it in his eyes.

And yet a matter of minutes later his cruel accusations had seemed to sweep all that away. Suddenly there had been only coldness in his eyes and bitter condemnation in every syllable he spoke, while she had felt herself thrown back emotionally to that time when she had believed that she had come to hate him.

It was not possible to love and hate simultaneously, so which of the two emotions was either of them really feeling? Hers was not the only head she longed to see into. At this moment she sensed that his was as mixed up as her own. Yet as she glanced at his profile as they sped through the snowscape, she felt a knot of anxiety tighten within her. For if he really despised her and she really loved him, how on earth would she be able to cope?

Her fists tightened nervously as cold fear washed through her, filling her with a dull sense of regret. For these past few years she had eschewed all real emotion and, though perhaps a little emptily, she had survived. This dam-burst of emotion exploding between them was threatening to tear her sanity to shreds.

And where was he taking her? She glanced around her, suddenly recognising the route they were taking. 'What are you up to?' She turned on him accusingly. 'Are you out of your mind, taking me back to Greystanes?'

'Can you think of a better place for a private discussion? I'm certainly not taking you back to your place.'

'But what about Evelyn? She'll be there.'

'Evelyn will have been in bed for hours. And if she isn't, don't worry, that's where I'll send her.' His fist banged the steering-wheel in sudden frustration. 'Damn it, it's my house! If I want to go there, I'll go there! I don't need anybody's damned permission!'

'I'd still rather we didn't go there,' Isla insisted, remembering that unhappy previous visit. 'If you insist on talking, we can talk in the car—although, as I told you before, there's really nothing to talk about.'

'There's everything to talk about.' He held her eyes, and, as the dark tawny gaze held hers for a moment, Isla thought she glimpsed through his grim expression a flicker of some more positive emotion.

Was it possible, she wondered, as he turned back to his driving, that he longed to heal this new rift as badly as she? For she could not deny that, through her still-seething anger, more than anything she was praying that it might be possible to recapture the closeness of just an hour ago. And maybe, just maybe, it could happen if both of them wanted it badly enough.

They were passing between the eagle-crested gateposts of Greystanes, then winding swiftly up the driveway to the heavy brass-studded front door.

Here and there from behind closed curtains cracks of light shone out into the night, while a set of lights out in the forecourt illuminated the front of the house. How nice, Isla thought wryly, to have a battery of servants to make the house ready for one's return.

A moment later she stepped behind him into the huge hall with its russet-red carpet and ancestral portraits hanging from the walls. It was just as she remembered it. Nothing had changed. But even as she opened her mouth to say so the words froze unspoken in her throat. For through an archway beyond the staircase had appeared a figure as unchanged as the décor itself.

The figure paused for a moment and frowned across at her, then turned her steely gaze on her son. 'Good evening, Rory. I'm sorry to surprise you. I didn't expect you to show up here—and I certainly didn't expect that you would have company.'

In the awkward fractional silence that followed Isla kept her eyes fixed on Elizabeth Buchanan as she continued her passage across the hallway. She had indeed changed little, Isla observed, her stomach clenching. She was as handsome and as hostile as eight years ago. And, though Greystanes no longer belonged to her, she had adroitly managed to make Isla feel just as unwelcome as she had before.

Then Rory spoke, addressing his mother. 'Isla and I were just about to have a nightcap.' His tone was controlled, devoid of emotion and yet with an uncertain ring about it. He paused. 'I, too, am surprised to find you here. Is there some problem at the cottage?'

Elizabeth beamed a smile of apology at her son. 'I'm afraid the central heating's broken down again and I can't get anyone to come and fix it till tomorrow. In the meantime I've installed myself in the blue room. I hope you don't have any objection?'

'Of course I don't,' Rory answered immediately. 'You must stay here at the house until the heating's been fixed. We can hardly have you freezing down at the cottage.'

Elizabeth smiled gratefully and took her son's arm. 'Thank you, my dear. What would I do without you?' Then she turned condescendingly towards Isla and enquired in a mock-friendly voice, 'What an unexpected pleasure. I understand you're down in London these days.'

Isla nodded politely, feeling her antipathy harden as she looked into the light brown eyes. This was the woman who had so opposed her relationship with Rory and whom she had always largely blamed for its demise. 'That's right,' she responded with careful politeness. 'I've been up visiting my parents for Christmas and New Year.'

'And are they well?' Elizabeth enquired, still smiling sweetly. 'I heard your father had been in hospital.'

Isla had no desire to discuss her father with Elizabeth. She answered a little brusquely, 'He's fine now, thank you. Both of them are.'

'In that case, I expect you'll be going back home soon? Now that there's nothing to keep you here.'

Subtlety had never been Elizabeth's strong point. She had never liked Isla and she had never shirked from showing it. And this was the woman, Isla thought with rising anger, whom Rory had allowed to influence him in the most crucial areas of his life. She had been opposed to Isla, so Rory had dropped her. She had approved of Evelyn, so he had made Evelyn his wife.

An uncontrollable fury went sweeping through her, a fury directed principally at herself. What on earth was she doing here, fooling herself that on the strength of the little chat they'd been planning to have all the problems between herself and Rory

could somehow, miraculously, be solved? As long
as there was Elizabeth there would be no solutions,
at least none that would be permitted to last. What
they had shared this afternoon was all they would
ever share. Elizabeth would see to that.

She looked the older woman straight in the eye.
'You're absolutely right. There's nothing more to
keep me. That's why I'll be going back south
tomorrow.' Then she turned to Rory to meet his
oddly distant gaze. 'I think we should skip that
nightcap, after all. I have a rather early start.'

Had she hoped he might ask his mother to leave
them, then insist Isla stay on to continue their discussion? If so, she was in for a disappointment, for
with barely a ripple in his composure he answered,
'You're right, that nightcap was not a good idea.
It's best I take you home right away.'

Then, pausing only to kiss his mother on the
cheek, he was leading Isla through the front door
to the waiting car.

CHAPTER TEN

THE journey from Greystanes back to Isla's parents' cottage was conducted at speed and in total silence. It was only as they drew up outside the cottage that Rory turned to her and asked, 'Are you absolutely sure you have to go back tomorrow?'

Isla answered without looking at him, 'I have a job to get back to.' She reached for the door-handle. 'Thank you for the lift.'

'Don't mention it.' She felt him smile coldly, then he stretched in front of her to push the door open. 'I hope you have a pleasant journey. I don't expect we'll be seeing one another again.'

'I don't expect we shall.' She stepped out hurriedly. 'Goodnight.'

'Goodbye.'

On that note of finality he was gone, almost before the car door had slammed shut.

And that was that. The end at last of a day of emotional upheaval and turmoil. Isla crept on tiptoe through to her bedroom, careful not to wake her parents, then undressed hurriedly and slipped into bed.

This time tomorrow she would be back in London. She closed her eyes and tried to feel pleased. After all the unexpected diversions of Strathallane she would be able to channel her thoughts once more into those areas of her life that were really important. For a start she must sort out her career.

She clutched the blankets to her chin and tried to feel enthusiastic about the weeks ahead. A new job was waiting for her, an exciting new challenge. All she had to do was choose which job to go for.

She sighed and rolled over and stared into the night, unable to summon up even a whisper of excitement. For all she cared about such things at the moment, she might as well make her choice with a piece of paper and a pin.

She chided herself silently. That was no way to think. It was the traumas of the day that were making her feel so negative. Once she was gone from here, back to normality, with Rory put behind her once and for all . . . But it was thoughts of Rory that kept crowding in on her. She had to fight to banish him from her mind.

What was it he had said? 'There were times when I needed you unbearably, times when I was desperate for someone to talk to, but you were never there.'

She thrust the thought from her. She must not think of him. To think of him would drive her mad.

She lay for a moment, trying to concentrate on tomorrow. The journey. London. Returning to her flat. But it was hopeless. He kept intruding, as though he were in the room with her. She simply could not drive him away.

She threw back the covers and stepped on to the carpet. A hot drink was what she needed. That would make her sleep.

With a sigh she pulled on her warm woollen robe, jammed her feet into her slippers and padded out into the corridor. In the kitchen she set a pan on the stove, poured in some milk and turned on the gas. A little honey and a shot of her father's New Year whisky wouldn't go amiss either, she decided wryly. She stirred the mixture up in a mug, then sat down at the kitchen table and took a sip. Then she closed her eyes, and, with the mug in both hands, leaned her chin against the rim.

What had he meant by it? I needed you unbearably. I needed you unbearably. But you were never there.

She felt a shiver run through her. He had said it with such passion that it was impossible to doubt the reproach was sincere. Yet she had rejected it, barely listening to it, when he had said it. It so went against all she had ever believed.

She took a deep breath, feeling it shudder through her. Was it possible she had been wrong about that too for all these years? During that period when he had taken over Buchanan's and she had believed he was slipping away from her, was it possible that the real truth was that she had failed him?

She could remember even now his terrible grief at the death of Niall, doubly terrible for coming so close after the death of his father, and she remembered, too, how his grief had frightened her. Had she allowed that fear to distort her vision of him, believing that his grief had somehow driven out his love for her? She had always, after all, been afraid of losing him, such a wild, free spirit had he been then.

It had never occurred to her that he might need her. She had allowed his grief to shut her out. And, besides, she had believed that Rory needed no one. That he was complete in himself, a rock of strength.

She frowned into her mug as the truth slowly dawned on her. She had grabbed at the possibility of that job in London simply because she had believed that he no longer wanted her and because her pride would not allow her to stay. And he, believing that the reason for her decision was that her ambition was stronger than her love for him, had been too proud to beg her to stay.

Isla swallowed drily. It was their pride that had destroyed them. Both had been too proud to plead.

She sat back in her chair and laid the mug down. And yet he had come to her in London, hoping to persuade her to go back home with him. And she might have gone, for she had prayed that he might follow her, but by then there had been the tragedy of the miscarriage, a further stumbling block between them.

A tear rolled down her cheek and fell to the kitchen table. Then another one followed. She wiped it away. She had needed him then, yet she had driven him from her, blaming him for his absence in her darkest hour.

She laughed bitterly now. What a fool she had been. How could she blame him when, until this very day, he had not known about the child?

So much pride. So many misunderstandings. So much left unspoken that should have been said. And each in his or her own way had been paying for all these omissions—Rory with his disastrous marriage, she with her lonely love-life—for eight long miserable years. Foolish pride had demanded a heavy price.

But eight years was long enough. Now the foolishness must end.

There was a rustle in the doorway and Isla glanced up to find her mother watching her with a look of concern. 'Are you all right, my dear? I was up to the bathroom and I saw the light.'

Isla smiled back at her mother reassuringly. 'Just a touch of insomnia. I've made myself a drink.' She drank it back quickly and rose to her feet. 'But I think it's time I was getting back to bed. Tomorrow's going to be a long, busy day.'

Isla parked the little Renault outside the Buchanan building and walked swiftly across the tarmac to the main door. It was snowing lightly, a swirl of delicate white flakes, and she brushed them quickly from her hair as she stepped into the carpeted entrance hall, then strode past Reception to the lifts at the back.

As on that first visit just two weeks ago, she knew exactly where she was going.

The lift doors opened when they reched the third floor and, feeling the faintest clench in the pit of her stomach, Isla stepped out and hurried along the corridor to the office with the ornate gold lettering on the door. She pushed the door open and stepped inside, casting a smile of recognition at the young secretary behind the desk.

'Good morning, Jackie. I'm sorry to barge in, but I want to have a word with Mr Buchanan.'

The girl smiled back at her. 'Good morning, Miss MacDonald. I'm afraid Mr Buchanan's in a meeting.' She glanced at her watch and rose to her feet. 'You can wait in his office if you like. He shouldn't be long and I know he wouldn't mind.'

Then, as Isla smiled gratefully, she added, 'I'll bring you a cup of coffee while you're waiting. Black, no sugar, if I remember rightly.'

Isla nodded as she stepped into Rory's private office. 'You remember rightly. Thanks, Jackie. That's very good of you.'

As the office door closed behind the young secretary, Isla let out a sigh to release the tension within her. Part of her was not at all sure she should be here. After all, she had intended to be on the train back to London. But another, stronger part of her was none the less determined to see through to the end the mission she had set herself.

Rory may not want to hear what she had come to say, but he was going to hear it anyway.

She had made the decision last night in the kitchen when everything had suddenly seemed so clear to her. For she had understood at last what lay behind his hostility, why he had accused her of selfishness, of caring only about herself. And out of fairness to both of them she planned to put him right. She had not left Strathallane because she did not love him. She had left because she loved him too much.

Restlessly now she paced the carpet, too nervous to sit down in one of the chairs. She was acutely aware that this latest revelation might not interest him in the least. Perhaps his antagonism was by now too deeply entrenched. But she knew she could not go back to London without at least trying to set the record straight.

And of course, in her heart, she could always hope that what she had come to say might actually matter to him. Yesterday she had sensed that he still cared at least a little—though who could guess at the true emotions of so complex a man? But, whether he cared or not, she at least had no more doubts as to what her own personal feelings were.

She loved him, pure and simple. She had always loved him. And no longer would she deny it or try to suppress it. She had already been doing that for far too long.

Hands thrust into the pockets of her navy cashmere coat, she paced her way to the edge of his desk, then stepped beyond it to frown out of the window. It's still snowing, she thought idly, finding the waiting a torture, then she turned away abruptly to let her eyes scan his desk. It looked huge and empty and meaningless without him. A little, she thought wanly, like my life.

It was just as she was about to step past the desk again that the silver-framed photograph that had caught her eye that first time momentarily caught her attention again. Only this time it was facing her. She could see the picture quite clearly, and for a moment, as she felt a flicker of recognition, her heart seemed to stop inside her breast. But then, before she could look more closely, the door opened and Rory stepped into the room.

He was wearing a dark grey suit, white shirt and claret tie. His black hair was brushed back from his forehead. And at the sight of him Isla felt her heart shrink with longing. How could she ever have dreamed of loving anyone else?

He was carrying a cup of coffee in one hand. He held it out to her. 'This is yours, I believe.'

Almost guiltily, Isla moved away from the desk and hurried towards him to take the cup. 'Thank you,' she mumbled, as he walked briskly past her and seated himself in the chair behind the desk.

He busied himself stowing some papers in a drawer as, feeling awkward, she perched on one of the high-backed chairs opposite him. And he did not deign to raise his eyes to look at her as he observed, 'I expected you to be on your way back to London by now. What brings you here? Have you more demands to make?'

The hostility she sensed in him was almost tangible. For a moment Isla was tempted just to turn and go. Then, as she gritted her teeth—she must not be put off!—she was tempted to reply that she had just been passing, that she had intended all along to catch a later train, but just in time she stopped herself. She was here to put right the mistakes that had been made, not to allow history to repeat itself—for suddenly she understood and sympathised with how Rory must have felt that time in London.

She took a deep breath. 'I have no demands to make. It's just that I couldn't leave without speaking to you,' she said.

He glanced up then, a trifle warily, she thought. 'I thought you said last night that we had nothing to talk about?'

'You're right, I did. But I was wrong. I think I've been wrong about a lot of things.'

He straightened and closed the drawer. 'I seem to be hearing things. I thought Isla MacDonald was never mistaken?'

Isla swallowed hard. 'I thought so, too. I'm a little like Rory Buchanan in that respect.'

Just for a moment his expression softened. She thought she saw the glimmer of a smile. 'So, what in particular did you want to tell me?'

Isla laid down her coffee-cup and clasped her hands in her lap. Then she straightened a little and looked straight at him. 'I want to tell you a whole load of things I should have told you years ago.' She caught her breath. 'Please don't interrupt. Just listen and hear what I have to say.'

He sat back in his chair, the tawny eyes fixing her. 'Go ahead. I'm listening,' he said.

The first few words were the most difficult to get out. After that the rest came easily. Scarcely stopping for breath, she recounted at length the whole sad story of eight years ago. She confessed the fears she'd always had of losing him, the feelings she'd had that he'd been pushing her from him and the desperation that had driven her to flee to London. And though her voice remained calm, as she came to the end of it the tears were streaming unashamedly down her cheeks.

She stared down into her lap, her fingers twisting together. 'You have no idea what a relief it is to get this off my chest. I've been bottling it all up inside me for years.'

Almost without her noticing, he had come out from behind the desk and was drawing up one of the high-backed chairs beside her. He lowered himself on to it and took her hands in his and when he spoke his voice was ragged with emotion. 'How could you ever have doubted that I loved you and needed you? Dear lord, Isla, you were my life.' He squeezed her trembling fingers and raised them to his lips. 'It almost destroyed me when you left for London.'

She raised bright violet eyes, brimming with tears, and looked back into his frowning face. 'It very nearly destroyed me, too. But I was driven by fear and insecurity. I suppose it was the insecurity of youth.'

Rory groaned deep in his throat as he pulled her to him. 'I should have known, I should have made it clear to you. But I was young, too. Young and thoughtless and irresponsible. I just took it for granted that you knew.'

But now he was being unfair to himself. Isla blinked away the tears and touched her fingers to his face. 'You had every right to take it for granted. You showered me with proof of your love at the start. It was only after Niall died and you were thrust into the chairmanship that I became afraid that you were starting to withdraw.'

As he opened his mouth to speak, she laid a finger on his lips and went on to finish what she had been about to say. 'But, Rory, nobody could blame you for that. You were out of your mind, thrown upside-down. You had too much to cope with to have to worry about me, too.'

'But I should have, Isla. I loved you. I owed it to you.'

'And I owed it to you to support you when you needed me, instead of selfishly demanding that you support me.' She kissed his face. 'I'm sorry for that now. I'd give anything to have done things differently.'

'And I'd give anything to have been with you at the time of the miscarriage.' He stroked her hair, his voice tight with remorse. 'That whole episode must have been a nightmare for you.'

'It was a nightmare.' Her voice choked a little. 'But, funnily enough, it was an enormous comfort to me that my sister's daughter Rebecca was born more or less at the same time that our child would have been born. In a strange way I've always felt that she was partly mine.'

'Poor darling.' He kissed her hair and held her close. 'I'll never forgive myself for not knowing you were pregnant.'

'How could you have known when I didn't tell you? The fault was mine. You've nothing to blame yourself for there.' She looked deep into his eyes. 'I've made so many mistakes, but through it all, though I tried my hardest to hate you, I never stopped loving you for a single minute.' She glanced away, suddenly embarrassed by her confession. 'Deep inside I think I always knew it, but I was too afraid to face it.'

He held her tightly in silence for a moment, then he drew back a little and frowned into her eyes. 'I have a confession, too,' he told her. Then he rose to his feet and crossed to the desk and picked up the silver-framed photograph. He stood before her and held it out to her, so that she could see clearly the image portrayed there. And yes, she realised, her heart leaping a little, it was precisely the photograph she had thought it was.

Rory was watching her, a warm smile on his face. 'It's sat there on my desk for years and no one, I'm sure, ever knew what it was. Just a rear view of two distant figures on horseback. Only you and I know better.'

Tears pricked Isla's eyes as she glanced down at the image. It was a picture that had been taken of herself and Rory at Kirkhaven Castle eight years ago as they were setting out on their pony-trekking holiday. The two of them had just spent their first night together. No two people had ever been happier or so much in love.

'And I thought it was a picture of Evelyn,' Isla murmured, her voice breaking to think he should so treasure that moment that he should keep it in a silver frame on his desk.

'Never, my darling. My love has always been yours.' He laid the picture back on the desk and drew her gently to her feet. 'I never really loved Evelyn. Not as I love you. I think the only reason I married her was to prove to myself that I could live without you.'

A sudden thought came to Isla. She had to say it. 'Not because your mother wished it?'

He leaned back a little, his eyes wide with astonishment. 'You don't seriously believe I would marry to please my mother?' Then a wry smile touched his lips. 'I know what you're thinking. You're remembering that she was always against us marrying. Well, take my word for it, she was against my marrying Evelyn, too. I suppose it's because I'm the only son she has left, she can sometimes be a little possessive.'

'But you said both your families were pushing you!'

'So they were—all with the exception of my mother. I have a score of uncles and aunts and cousins. They were the ones who were urging me into it.' He shook his dark head. 'But their influence was zero. If anything, all their pushing almost made me back out.'

He smiled a wry smile. 'I thought you knew me better. I make my own decisions, my own mistakes. And that's the way it will always be.' He kissed her. 'Only now I shall expect a little help from you. As my wife I think that's the least you can do for me.'

Isla felt her heart turn over. Her breath caught in her throat. 'Is that a proposal?'

He caught her chin with his fingers and looked long into her eyes. 'It's a proposal all right, and you have no choice but to accept it. You realise there's no way I'm going to let you go?' Softly, he kissed her, making her heart melt. 'You're going to stay right here and you're going to marry me. For one thing,' he smiled, 'you may be carrying my child again. Perhaps you hadn't thought of that?'

But Isla had thought of it and the thought had warmed her, for she had known that even if she were to lose Rory forever a part of him would always be with her.

She looked into his face. 'Is that why you want to marry me?'

'I want to marry you because I love you. Because I can no longer envisage a life without you. Whether now or later, you will have my child. That is something I can promise you.'

Isla held his gaze. 'And what if I hadn't come here? What if I'd gone back to London this morning as I'd intended?'

He raised one dark eyebrow. 'That would have held things up a little. But only by a matter of hours.' With a secret smile he reached into his jacket pocket and drew out an airline ticket to London. 'I planned to fly down this afternoon and meet you off the train—then turn you right round again and bring you back here.'

Isla laughed delightedly. 'I'm almost sorry I missed that. I've always secretly longed for you to whisk me off somewhere.'

He embraced her lovingly. 'I'll whisk you off anywhere. Just name your destination. But only if you promise to be my wife.'

Isla looked into his eyes, her soul burning with love for him. 'I'll be your wife. It's all I've ever wanted. And you don't really have to whisk me off anywhere. All I ask of you is that you love me.'

He leaned to kiss her long and deeply. 'That's easily granted. I've always loved you. Even if you asked me to I couldn't stop now.' Then his arms were around her, as though he would never release her, and she was melting against him, alight with happiness. Finally, at long last, she was back where she belonged.

That August Strathallane saw a triple celebration.

For August was the month when the new magazine was launched upon a delighted public. It was also the occasion of its editor's twenty-seventh birthday and, most special of all, on the first day of the month Isla's doctor confirmed what she had already suspected. Buchanan of Strathallane's heir was due to arrive in time for Christmas.

The last few months had been quite remarkable.

First, just a week or so into the new year, Evelyn had taken the town by storm by announcing at a local parish meeting that she and Rory were divorced and that the child she was carrying was not his. Then, before the parishioners had had time to catch their breath, she had flown off to marry the new man in her life, leaving the way open for Rory and Isla to publicly announce their engagement.

The wedding had taken place on St Valentine's day, a bright snowy day, unforgettably magical, then Rory had whisked them both off to Bermuda for a three-week dream honeymoon in the sun.

But now it was the evening of that twenty-seventh birthday party, less than an hour before the celebrations were due to begin.

Isla regarded herself in the bedroom mirror, pleased and happy with what she saw there. In the floor-length midnight-blue velvet dress she looked almost as wonderful as she felt. And there was a bloom in her cheeks and a sparkle in her eyes that told the whole world she was sublimely happy.

She turned to face the figure behind her, looking tall and splendid in a formal black suit. 'I reckon we ought to go downstairs now. We mustn't be late to greet our guests.'

Rory came towards her. 'You're looking beautiful.' He slipped his arms round her and kissed her hair. 'I don't give a damn about our guests. I'd just as soon stay here and make love to you.'

His words sent a tight little flutter through her. Just the thought of his lovemaking made her blood dance. She too would gladly have abandoned the party just to spend a magical few hours in his arms.

But it was her birthday party and he had gone to enormous trouble to organise a special evening for her. She glanced down at her wrist and the solid gold bracelet that he had given her on her eighteenth birthday all those years ago. He had promised her a gold charm for every birthday and a special one on the day that they married—and that promise, like all the others, he had fulfilled. The eight missing charms had now been added, with an emerald-studded star to match her engagement ring as the symbol of their wedding day.

And there would be an even more special one to add to that on the day that their first baby was born.

Isla sighed and leaned against him, sliding her arms around his neck, her soul awash with a sense of wonder at how fate had turned her life around. Who, just a few short months ago, would ever have believed she could wind up this happy? Yet here she was, married to the man she loved and very soon to have his baby. There was not a cloud on her horizon and all the nightmares had finally ceased. Even the problem of her new mother-in-law, she thought with a smile, had proved, after all, not to be a problem.

She looked up at Rory with a mischievous smile. 'That was good of your mother,' she told him, teasing, 'to surprise me with such a beautiful bouquet of flowers.'

'You shouldn't be surprised. I told you she would learn to love you, just as you're learning to love her.'

Isla giggled. 'Let's not exaggerate. But I'm learning to *like* her, I can't deny that.'

And much to her own astonishment it was actually true. Once Elizabeth had accepted her son's determination to marry Isla her entire attitude to her future daughter-in-law had changed. And Isla, too, had revised her opinion, knowing that she'd been wrong for all those years to blame Elizabeth for the break-up between herself and Rory. Thanks to their pride and their immaturity they had managed that all by themselves.

But now it was as though all that had never happened. The past was behind them and the future was secure. She looked into the face of her handsome husband and told him simply, 'I love you so much.'

He pulled her close. 'I love you, too. And I intend to demonstrate just how much on the banks of Loch Lomond at midnight tonight.'

Isla blinked at him. 'Loch Lomond?'

'Don't tell me you've forgotten?'

She shook her head and kissed his face. 'On the banks of Loch Lomond was where you first made love to me. How could I forget a thing like that?'

'Then it's a date?' He grinned and winked at her.

She kissed him again. 'I wouldn't miss it for the world.'

And as he drew her softly into his arms her heart was as big as a football in her chest. This wonderful man was the very same man whom she had fallen in love with all those years ago. And now, at last, he belonged to her and she was the happiest, luckiest woman alive.

HARLEQUIN

Romance®

announces

THE BRIDAL COLLECTION

one special Romance
every month,
featuring
a Bride, a Groom and a Wedding!

Beginning in May 1992
with
The Man You'll Marry
by Debbie Macomber

WED-1

Following the success of WITH THIS RING,
Harlequin cordially invites you to enjoy the
romance of the wedding season with

BARBARA BRETTON
RITA CLAY ESTRADA
SANDRA JAMES
DEBBIE MACOMBER

A collection of romantic stories that celebrate the joy,
excitement, and mishaps of planning that special day
by these four award-winning Harlequin authors.

**Available in April at your favorite Harlequin
retail outlets.**

THTH

HARLEQUIN PROUDLY PRESENTS A
DAZZLING CONCEPT IN ROMANCE FICTION

One small town,
twelve terrific love stories.

TYLER—GREAT READING…GREAT SAVINGS…
AND A FABULOUS FREE GIFT

Each book set in Tyler is a self-contained love story; together, the twelve novels stitch the fabric of the community.

By collecting proofs-of-purchase found in each Tyler book, you can receive a fabulous gift, ABSOLUTELY FREE! And use our special Tyler coupons to save on your next Tyler book purchase.

Join us for the third Tyler book, WISCONSIN WEDDING by Carla Neggers, available in May.

Janet Dailey
Americana

Janet Dailey's perennially popular Americana series
continues with more exciting states!

Don't miss this romantic tour of America through
fifty favorite Harlequin Presents novels, each one set
in a different state, and researched by Janet and her
husband, Bill.

A journey of a lifetime in one cherished collection.

May titles   **#31 NEW MEXICO**
                              Land of Enchantment

                           #33 NEW YORK
                              Beware of the Stranger